TALON

MARKED

BY

SUE-ELLEN

PASHLEY

First published by Deadset Press in 2024.

© Deadset Press 2024

Cover design Copyright © Austin P. Sheehan.

Edited by Austin P. Sheehan.

isbn: 978-0-6450228-9-6

For Adrian, always.

And for everyone who's always dreamed of befriending a dragon!

Acknowledgement of Country:

In the spirit of reconciliation, Deadset Press acknowledges the Traditional Custodians of country throughout Australia and their connections to land, sea and community. We pay our respect to their Elders past and present and extend that respect to all Aboriginal and Torres Strait Islander peoples today.

CONTENTS

CHAPTER ONE

The dragon shoots low over my head, black and blue scales glinting in the early morning sun. In desperation, I scramble for a hiding space in the scrubby forest, heart slamming in my chest, trying not to think, not to breathe.

Gods, why had I come so close to the dragon border? Stupid! I'd thought it a risk worth taking when I made the decision eight days ago, shaving almost two weeks off my journey to Axiam. Two weeks! And yet, now, with the vastness of the dragon's shadow over me and the terror that it will sense me, control me . . . I cower lower still.

And then, it's gone.

I wait to hear our soldiers' war cries. They must be close if the dragon is here, in our territory. I've been avoiding the army camps, knowing they'll send me back to safety should they see me, and have been skirting the areas of forest reduced to ash by the dragons' flames, conscious that no cover will be found there, from the army or the dragons.

I need to get to Axiam though. It's the last place my brother, Gaiven, was seen, and that information is already at least two months old. Still, it's the next piece of the puzzle. One I'm desperate to complete before I grow old and grey and wonder what happened to the last of my happy family. The people who made me feel loved and safe before everything changed.

Safe.

I can only just remember how that felt, like a half-forgotten memory of the peppermint biscuits my mother used to make for birthdays.

When the silence continues, I rise to a crouch, hidden still, worried it might be a ruse.

Nothing moves.

I lick my lips, creating moisture in my dry mouth, and try to decide what to do now, even if my brain is telling me to run, run, run. Away, anywhere, run.

Slowly, I stand to my full height, adjusting the backpack on my shoulders. Nothing else moves. And my decision is made. Trudging on, I avoid the worst of the mud that clings to my boots and slows me down. I've come too far to turn back now, just because of one dragon that's probably long gone. I try not to think about how many more I might encounter.

Stopping for a moment to pick some of the blue cornbow flowers growing in a patch of sun, I suck the thick, sweet middle out before discarding them again. Our mother used to pick them to decorate the table but I'm thankful for them now for a different reason. They've been my main source of nutrition for the last eight months. Not ideal but enough to keep me going between the rare times when something more substantial is available.

The thundering noise of forest destruction ahead of me is a shock in the quiet morning stillness. I'm down behind the scant protection of a tree before my brain has time to make sense of it. My heart is stuttering in my chest as if the only reason it hasn't run scared is that it's constrained by my ribs.

I stay crouched, trying to figure out what the hell it was, but when the long silence is broken by the noise of birds and insects, there's no reason to stay hidden. And yet . . . the noise came from the direction I have to head to reach Axiam. Not unless I want to go for a swim in the river. Which I don't. At this time of year, it's swollen and angry and cold and I'm not stupid enough to think I'll be able to survive walking in this weather in wet clothes.

Standing here isn't going to change anything, and I don't have time to be a coward, so I blow out a frustrated breath and start walking, taking care to stick closer to the tree line than the path. There's no point in taking stupid risks.

I walk for ten minutes before the noise reaches me. It's like the sound of a hundred people breathing at once – blowing out a breath and sucking it back in, all at the same time. My legs tense and adrenalin courses through my veins, making me jittery. Is it the dragon, brought down by our forces? It must be. But then, where are they? Why aren't they here, finishing it off?

I wait for an hour, holding myself so still my muscles ache, and yet, no one comes. The cliffs on one side of me and the river on the other give me no choice, except if I want to turn around and I can't do that; I won't. Not when I'm so close. And it might *not* be the dragon.

I bite down on the inside of my cheek, wishing I had someone else with me to push me forward. Someone else to be brave enough to take the first step. I shake my head, the indecision playing through my mind annoying me. Creeping forward, I step on the sodden undergrowth to stop the mud sucking at each footfall and giving me away.

And then, there it is, mud and torn up trees in front of it like a lumpy pillow from where it crashed into the ground. The sound from earlier.

A dragon.

The black and blue one which flew over me. This is the closest I've ever been to one and it's still a good hundred metres from where I stand. Its eyes are shut and one of its front legs is at an odd angle. And it's breathing. In and out, great big bursts of air that blow up the dirt and leaves in front of it. Alive then.

Shit.

I know you are there, human. Show yourself.

The voice echoes in my head, swelling like it's filling up all the spaces in my brain, not giving me room to think. I grip the tree beside me, trying not to give into the command. It's harder than I

4

thought. Harder than what my father told us when we sat around the fire, talking about dragons and their ability to compel and subjugate humans, bending us to their will. Of course, that was before the great dragon-human war, when they stopped being aloof neighbours and became a horrifying nightmare instead.

Come forward.

I take one step and then grit my teeth, holding back, pushing back – resisting. It's like trying to hold myself still while waves crash in on me, dragging at my body. It's harder to resist when you're one-on-one with them, the army tells us in the flyers they send out. Much easier to not give in when the command is spread over a group. That's why the King is never alone. And that's why we've managed to keep fighting, despite their size and fire and mind power – because we have the sheer numbers to dilute their influence.

The dragon grumbles, a sound from deep in the earth, rumbling up, vibrating my bones, my organs, my blood.

I do not have time for your stubbornness. Come!

The command in his voice is too much and panic flares in my chest, my brain, but has no impact on my actions. Even though I try to resist, my feet move forward like I no longer control them, until I'm only metres from it, its breath hot on my legs, its dragon scent overwhelming me – an odd mix of fire and smoke and pine and earth. It's golden eye, as big as my head, surveys me, like it's

5

taking stock.

What is your name?

I hold it back, swallow it down, but the word is drawn out of my throat like a piece of metal compelled towards a magnet.

"Sage."

Sage. The dragon lifts its head slightly, revealing a long cut starting at its throat, travelling down to its chest, where some of the scales have been torn away, seeping dark red blood. Its voice has the same tightness to it my father's had when he'd been injured and was trying not to show his pain, and I can't help rejoicing in it. *I am injured. I require your help.*

Shaking my head, like our long-gone horse when she'd attempt to shake off her bridle, I try to rid myself of its power pressing on my brain.

"No. I'm not helping you." Those five words take enormous effort, and I'm panting like I've run for hours. The panic raging through me slams against the dragon's control and my brain feels as if it's being split in two.

Stop resisting! I do not have time!

"Good. Die. One less dragon to kill us."

He roars then. A roar which fills every inch of space around us, pushing in on me until it's as if my skull is going to cave in from the pressure. I drop to my knees, hands over my ears, although it's of no help. On and on it goes. When it stops, my ears ring still, taking away all the other sounds around me.

Come closer.

There's no pretence of resistance anymore. There's nothing left in me. I stand and walk forward until, if I lifted my hand, I'd be able to touch its cheek; feel the scales under my fingers.

I am sorry to do this to you but there is no other way.

It brings one of its talons up close to its mouth and breathes out a small flame, the heat of it warming my face to the point of being unbearable. And yet, I can't move away. I stand there, watching the talon glow red with the heat, knowing what's coming, even if I don't want to believe that it's happening to me.

Run, my brain tells me. Run, run, run!

But still, I stand there.

And the talon is moving towards my face, closer, closer . . .

I am sorry, it says again but its words mean nothing. They're empty, because it's going to do it to me anyway.

The talon touches my cheek, burning hot, the scent of singed flesh filling my nostrils. The dragon's control of my brain, coupled with the pain, overwhelms me, drowning me, until there's nothing but the darkness that takes me away.

CHAPTER TWO

The heat of the fire warms my back and I sigh, eyes still shut as I lay on the firm ground. It's been a long time since I enjoyed a fire. They're too dangerous with dragons around.

Dragons!

My eyes fly open and I scramble to my feet, pounding heart pushing me to move, move, move! And as much as I'd like to listen to it; to make myself safe somehow, I hesitate, taking stock of my surroundings; looking for anything familiar.

The rough stone of high cliffs hem me in, the walls so tall, the well stoked fire doesn't conquer the shadows.

"About time you woke up."

The voice belongs to a man – a stranger – sitting on the other side of the flames and I dart behind a larger rock on my left, putting it between us, not sure if he's a threat. Not sure of anything.

My fingers grip the hard stone, as if it's providing me strength, and my voice, when I manage to make it work, comes out as a harsh croak. "Who are you?"

"Bex."

That tells me nothing and I'm about to ask another question when he turns his head to look me square on and I see it on his cheek, bright in the glow of the fire. The mark of a dragon's talon. The sign that you're no longer your own person; that you've been subjugated by a dragon.

Without thinking, my hand goes to my own cheek and I feel it; the skin taut and numb to my touch, like it no longer belongs to me.

My own talon mark.

A sob escapes me and I cover my mouth, trying to stop any more following. I don't have time to fall into that dark place. I need to stay strong. Focused.

Bex looks back at the fire but his voice still carries to me. "It's a shock, first time feeling it there, isn't it? At least, that's how it was for me. I couldn't get my head around it. It's not as bad as you think though, belonging to a dragon."

A flicker of anger flares in my gut but I don't use my energy to stoke it. If he's stupid enough to think being the slave of a dragon is okay, then good luck to him. But not me. Never. I'd rather die!

My pack is leaning on the wall behind me, just at the edge of the light. Bex doesn't turn as I grab it and strap it to my back. I watch him, expecting that at any moment, he'll get up and stop me. Working for the dragons . . .

I hold myself tall. "Which way is out?"

He looks at me, holding my gaze for a second, before looking away again, as if I'm of no consequence. That he couldn't care if I stayed or not. "To your left. That's the quickest way out of the ravine."

I turn, and then stop, even though my head is telling me to get out, get out, get out! While I still can. Before the dragon returns.

"Come with me." The words rush out of my mouth. I don't know why I say them except, in some perverse way, he reminds me of my brother. It must be his dark eyes, because he's older than Gaiv and stockier. And yet, he's still human.

He laughs. It chokes out of him like he's forgotten how to do it. "You won't get far. You're bonded with Sahva now, no matter how much you hate the thought of it. There's no way to undo it or wish it away. He'll find you. It doesn't make any difference where you hide, how fast you run . . . the mark means he'll know where you are. Every time."

My hand goes up to touch my cheek again and I shake my head. "No. There has to be a way. There must be."

He looks at me once more and I see the truth in his eyes. "Four. That's how many times I tried to get away. And that's how many times Hevil's found me. Without having to try very hard. And each time, he's commanded me to come. So, I came. Because that's all there is."

I don't want to believe him. He must be wrong. And yet, I know he's telling the truth. As much as I've been trying to ignore it, I can feel the dragon's presence in the back of my mind, like an out of reach itch.

"I need to try," I say, but it comes out as a whisper.

He shrugs. "If you have to. But it's not going to get you anywhere. And it'll probably make him angry."

The thought of the dragon being angry and what it could do stirs my stomach into a whirlpool of despair. Gods, how could this have happened? Isn't it enough I've lost my whole family, my home, everything that made me who I was? And now, I'm the slave of a dragon. Captured for the rest of my life.

And that's when the thought comes to me; a dark thought to match the darkness of night. Would I be better off ending my life? Finishing it, rather than having to live like this? Although then, who'd look for Gaiven? He'd have no family left. No one looking for him, wanting to protect him. He wouldn't know what had happened to me.

I'm not sure if it's because I'm still there or if he can see the expression on my face but Bex starts to talk again.

"At the start of the war, ten years ago. That's when Hevil marked me. I was delivering ale to a brewery and I came across him, injured, nearly dead. My horse kept shying away from the road we had to go down but I made her go. Hevil ate her, once he'd marked me, to regain his strength. I was sad about that for a long time – she was a good horse. Didn't deserve that ending, although at least it was fast. The first year was when I kept trying to get away. Tried to kill myself too. Figured I'd be better off dead than doing what a dragon wants."

His words jolt me and my breath catches in my throat like it's become solid. I don't want to ask but the words are out of my mouth before I can stop them.

"What happened?"

"I threw myself off the highest cliff I could find, straight onto rocks."

"And you didn't die?"

He sighs. "What do you know about dragons?"

I hesitate in answering, wanting to block my ears against his words like a child escaping taunting in the playground. Because all I know is what we've been told. By my father, the King, the army – and yet, it feels like his question is loaded. As if he knows information I don't. Things I maybe don't want to hear. Things that are going to make me feel like I'm betraying our kind. Betraying my family.

"I know they've killed hundreds, thousands of us. Women, children, men; they don't care. I know they can enslave us just with their voice and their talon mark. Like they've done to you." And to me. Although I don't say that out loud.

He does a half nod, half shrug. "Yes. All of that's true. But there are two sides to every story."

"So, what's their side?" My words are filled with rage but it's not really anger – it's fear. I don't want to know; don't want to hear about their experience, their reasons for killing humans and ruining so many lives that our land's no longer our safe refuge. I just want to keep hating them and get away to find my brother.

Bex is silent while he slips another log onto the fire, the flame sending sparks into the air. I should go. Now! Before he talks again! My legs won't comply though.

He doesn't answer my question though. Instead, he gets up and walks around the fire, closer to me.

"I'm going to show you something." He watches me for a moment until I nod and I have to steel myself not to take a step back when he unbuttons his shirt. His skin, a mixture of oranges and yellows and black shadows in the firelight, is marked with scars – a large one, running the length of his torso – and smaller ones, like my mother's cross stitch gone wrong.

"What happened?"

"I got most of these when I jumped off the cliff. Hevil saved me."

"What do you mean?"

"When he marked me," he said, doing his shirt back up, "it was to save himself. Like I said, he was injured. Close to death. When he bonded with me, it . . . fixed him. Made him stronger. He was whole again."

I think of the dragon who marked me, of the blood, of how injured it was, and shut my eyes, sick with the thought of it. "We make them stronger?"

"Yes. But they also make us stronger. I didn't die when I jumped, although I should've. And Hevil fixed me. Made me whole again. He didn't have to. There wasn't a reason for him to save me. If I die, it doesn't mean he will. He'll be the same as he was before – a little weaker, perhaps, but still whole. He did it because of our bond. Chose it because he *wanted* to save my life. And I've never tried to get away again."

I step back, away from the look in his eyes. The look that says he cares for the creature who enslaved him. Has truly bonded with him.

"You're a traitor!" The panic spiking in my chest makes me spit the words out at him, as if they're laced with a poison that'll shut him up. "I'll never stop trying to get away. I'll kill them, kill you if I have to."

Bex looks at me in silence, a slow nod his only movement, as if he's telling me he's been where I am, felt these things and that, in the end, none of it mattered. Then he sits next to the fire again. I don't know what I expected but it wasn't this calm, detached demeanour in the face of my threat. It holds me there, destabilised again.

"Did you hear me?"

His eyes flick to mine before going back to the fire. He rubs his hands together and holds them out to the flame. "Sahva, your dragon, is waiting at the end of the ravine for you."

14

Sahva. It has a name. And it's out there. Waiting for me. Waiting for me! Gods, oh Gods. The dread overwhelms me, weighing me down, crushing me until I'm gasping for air. And then, suddenly, it's gone and all I feel is peace, as if somebody, or something, has flicked a switch in my brain.

Come to me.

And I go because I have to. I need to face him. Sahva. The dragon I made stronger through this horrific bond.

CHAPTER THREE

The dawn light is just lightening the sky when I leave the ravine. He's there, his tail curled around his legs, wings tucked against his back, head low. Relaxed. Like he doesn't fear me.

He should.

Sage. He says my name with what sounds like affection and I hate it, but the peaceful feeling is hard to shake.

"Don't do that!"

What?

"Say my name. Control my emotions." I know it's him. It has to be.

You would prefer to be angry? Panicked?

"I prefer to be me! Not controlled by a dragon."

And the calmness goes. Just like that. Anger doesn't fill its place like I thought it would. Instead, I feel bone-numbingly tired, as if trying to resist his control and feel my true emotions has been too much for my body, my mind, and they're exhausted.

Sit.

I don't even bother to fight it. I don't have the strength. Dropping the pack from my shoulders, I sink to the ground, leaning against a rock. He watches me, a long blink covering his golden eye for a moment, giving me a chance to ask the question waiting on my tongue.

"Why did you do this to me?"

He rumbles, deep in his throat, but it's not like the one in the forest. This one is gentle, sorrowful.

I am sorry. I did not wish to do this. But there was no other way. Without you, I would have died. It is the one commonality between human and dragons, I think – neither willingly go to our deaths.

I remember then. Remember he told me he was sorry while he was doing it. And yet, it still happened. I'm marked.

"Take it away. Please. Let me go. You don't need me anymore." My voice catches but I keep the tears at bay. Just.

He lowers his head further, his snout only a few metres from my legs. *If I could, I would. But there is no way to undo it, once the bond is complete.*

I don't want to; the thought of showing my vulnerabilities to this dragon is terrible, but I can't stop the tears from coming. They roll down my cheeks, dripping onto my shirt and leather chest guard, both of which have seen better days.

"What does that mean for me?"

The dragon – Sahva – huffs and lays his head on the grass and dirt, still watching me. *It means you are mine and I am yours. Forever.*

Forever. The word echoes in my head and I can't even fathom what that means . . . It must just be a figure of speech; the words a priest would say in a marriage ceremony. Only unlike this, that's a choice people have made.

I don't know how long we sit there, me crying, him lying there watching me with eyes far more gentle and understanding than I could've imagined. He is a dragon. The enemy. The hated. The reason all but one of my family are dead. And yet, right now, I'm too exhausted to find the hate in me.

I don't know how I feel.

#

The sun is higher in the sky when I pull myself together. Enough, at least, that I'm not crying anymore.

You are hungry.

Anger flairs in my chest that he knows without me having to say anything but he's right. I don't know how long it's been since I've eaten anything more nutritious than cornbow flowers; how long I was unconscious after he marked me.

You need food. Some meat, I think, to restore your energy.

As he stands, wings outstretched and tail unwinding, a wave of awe and fear washes over me. He is majestic and terrifying. And beautiful. I'm full of so many emotions, my insides feel like they're being pulled in every direction, making me. . . thin.

Sahva flaps his massive wings, the down current swirling up the dust, and I cover my face. And then, he is in the air. Gone.

I'm alone. No Bex. No dragon. And all I can think of is my brother. My only family. Only fourteen when I last saw him.

Fifteen now, if he's still alive. Still a boy. I feel the guilt of him not having parents as I did and, while I know it's not my fault, that familiar ache - the ache that's kept me company for the last nine years and six months - washes back over me and I need to protect him, as I've always tried to.

And even though it's a stupid idea; Bex's warnings still twist in my brain and I have no idea where I am, I start to run. Run and run and run. Before my logical brain can stop me.

The low bushes tear at my clothes, scrape at my skin, but still I run.

I have no idea in what direction I'm going, but still I run.

And knowing Sahva will find me, but still . . . I run.

I have no choice. I have to try.

The sun is high when my body can't run anymore, although my brain is telling me to keep going. The cornbows are growing at the edge of a small stream and I fall to my knees in front of them, sucking the nectar and flesh from seven of them before looking around. There's a farm house sitting low on a hill across the stream. There are people there, moving around, living their lives, although it's too far away to make out details. People though, who can tell me where I am, maybe give me some supplies. Help me escape.

I take a moment to scoop river water into my mouth and wash the dirt and blood from my face. The shiny edges of the mark under my fingers remind me of the danger I'm in and I pull my hair around so it covers my mark; scared and angry all over again at the dragon and what he's done to me.

There's a log further up, spanning the river, and I balance across it, then make my way up the hill. The lack of food, and the energy I've used, has caught up with me, making every footstep heavy. I don't stop.

A young girl is playing with her doll at the door of the house and as I get closer, she stops playing and watches me, her face a blank mask. The war has had this effect on everyone. Distrust is evident everywhere, even of our own people. Not because of the dragons, but because desperation and scarcity can make for some evil deeds.

"Hello," I say as I approach. "Are your parents here?"

The sound of my voice alerts her mother, and within seconds the woman is behind her daughter, a hand on her shoulder. A protective guardian. Her hair is pulled back tight from her face and her shirt and pants need mending but then, mine are in a worse state. Her chest guard looks better though, so they must be doing okay.

"What do you want?"

"Food. If you have any to spare. I'm happy to work for it, whatever you need. And directions. I got . . . attacked. I don't know where I am."

Her face softens at my words. Not enough that I think I'm going to be taken in to the bosom of their family, but enough that she might help me. Maybe.

She jerks her head toward a building to the right of the house. The stables. My heart sinks before she has the words out but I know I'll do it, even if it's the job I hate most.

"The pig's stye needs mucking out."

I nod, trying not to let my feelings show on my face. To have food and information, I'm willing to do almost anything. "Okay." I turn to go and then stop. "Can you tell me where I am?"

"Estawall is about an hour south. The border to the dragon lands is half a day's walk that way." She nods her head in the direction I came from, eyes narrowed.

Estawall! My heart sinks. It's on the southern coast; at least four weeks walk from Axiam, and that's going at a good pace with no trouble along the way and no stops to work for food. The ravine I woke up in must've been on the dragon side of the border. The dragon has ripped me from my brother all over again, and echoes of the panic that swamped me the morning eight months ago when I'd woken and found Gaiv's bedroll empty, make my hands shake.

The dragon! Sahva!

He did this. I was so close and he did this! Another reason to hate him.

The anger swirls in my stomach like a whirlwind, spinning its way up my chest, up to my mouth, wanting to push its way out, filling me, consuming me. And all the time, the mother and her daughter watch me. Judging me.

I stand taller, pushing my hair back without even thinking. Until their expressions change. Their eyes are glued to my cheek and the colour drains from the woman's face. With hurried fingers, I brush my hair forward again, smoothing it down. It's too late.

She grabs a backstaff from beside the door, its long blade gleaming in the sunlight, and shoves it towards me. "Get away! Go! Piece of filth. Traitor!"

I stumble back, only just keeping my balance. "Please. No. I need your help. I have to get away. Help me!"

She spits at the ground between us, barely missing me. "Talon marked. Talon marked! Go. Go! Before you bring your dragon to kill us all."

She thrusts the blade at me again and gets my collarbone, drawing blood. Not deep but the pain that crashes into me isn't from the wound. It's from the realisation I'm no longer a part of my society. I don't fit in. I'll never be able to find Gaiv. In marking me, Sahva has ostracized me. He's killed me, even if I'm still breathing.

I turn and run. Back into the bush. Away from the border. Although I have no idea where to go now.

I run, not aware of my surroundings until I stumble over a tree root and my body scrapes across the dirt and leaves and rocks. And there I lay, my legs curling up under me, sobbing in great wracking breaths until my ribs almost break under the pressure. And when the sobs stopped, I still lay there. What's the point in moving? I may as well die here. In the dirt.

CHAPTER FOUR

The sky is staining to black when he finds me, although he's known where I was for a while. I've felt him the whole time, sitting there in the back of my brain. Waiting. Giving me space. Letting me feel the emotions rather than stopping them like he did before. And feeling all of it with me. I know all of this, although I don't want to know or care.

Sahva lands in the clearing in front of me, the soft thuds of his feet telling me where he is even if I can't see him. I still don't move.

He moves around me, gusting a flame from his mouth, the wood crackling as it catches fire. The smell of meat cooking fills the air, surrounding me. My traitor stomach rumbles, and saliva floods my mouth.

Come. There's no force in the word. It's gentle. Caring.

No. Leave me. Let me die. But I don't say this out loud. I lay there, still unable to move.

Come, Sage. Come. Eat.

He waits for me. Minutes? Hours? I don't know how long it is but he sits there. Patient. Waiting.

When my body won't listen to my smashed heart anymore, I get to my feet, unsteady. Weak. Like the newborn calves my father raised on our farm. Sahva doesn't move as I come towards him. I'm no longer angry or sad. Or anything. I am numb. Detached.

The deer he caught and cooked for me is on a pile of leaves, warm and fragrant, and I thump to the ground in front of it, tearing pieces off and putting them in my mouth, though I taste nothing. It could be soil for all the enjoyment I get from it. But it fills my stomach, and then I lay down on the ground and shut my eyes, hoping to never have to open them again.

#

The darkness is filled with fire, roars and screams, and I scramble to my feet before my brain has time to fully awaken. It's all chaos, but – like a picture coming into focus – it starts to make sense. There are people. People everywhere. With backstaffs, bows and knives. And there is Sahva. Flaming. Killing. Killing them while they cut him with their knives.

"Stop." My mouth is dry and the word croaks out. I try again and it's stronger this time. Louder. "Stop. Stop!"

I don't know who I'm yelling at though. The humans? The dragon?

Sage! Run! Run!

Before I can move, a man lunges at me, his backstaff going for the killing blow. Trying to kill *me*! The shock makes me stumble and that's what saves my life. The life I don't know if I want anymore. His blade hits the ground next to me and when he brings it back up to strike again, hatred is in his eyes. The same hatred the woman had. The blade comes down, the fire around us

25

adorning it with orange and yellow flecks. It's almost at my neck when I roll out of its way.

I'm not sure why, except suddenly, I'm not ready to die. Not like this. Not now.

There has to be more.

And then Sahva whips his tail around and the man's head disappears, his body crashing to the ground beside me. I swallow down the nausea and struggle to my feet, grabbing the backstaff which is still in his hands and holding it out in front of me. The noise has stopped though and there's no one left. The dragon has killed them all.

Sage, we must leave. There will be more. You must climb on me.

It's not a command this time, but I do it anyway. I'm not ready to be a dragon's slave but I'm also not willing to die because of what Sahva chose to do to me. And I will if I stay here.

Sahva holds his front leg out and I scramble up, settling into the crevice between his neck and body, holding on to one of the bony protrusions that travel up to his head.

And then, we're lifting in great surges which nearly rock me off, until he's clear of the trees and soars over the forest. Sahva was right. We are still in danger. There's another group of people in a burnt-out clearing, running after Sahva, shouting words that get lost in the wind, all the while knowing they have no chance of catching us.

We fly until numbness takes my fingers, my toes, my nose. The coldness has seeped into my bones and it's only because I'm pressing my lips together that my teeth aren't chattering.

The sun touches the horizon and rises through the sky and still we continue to fly. I shift, over and over, trying to relieve the stress on my body until finally he lands next to a small stream. After I relieve myself, I drink until my stomach is swollen, before sucking the goodness from the cornbows growing there.

We must continue. There's no room for argument in his command and I want to cry as I climb onto his back again, my body and mind sore.

At some point, I fall asleep, and every part of me is stiff and cold when I wake.

We are almost there.

I don't ask where 'there' is. I have only just enough brain power to stay on Sahva's neck. We fly over great swathes of swampy land, small islands peeping out of the brackish water as we head towards the ocean. When he lands, there's no graceful dismount from me. I slide down his scales, landing in a heap on the ground and it's only then that I look around. We're on a beach and in the early morning sun, rocks are jutting out into the ocean, curving around to make a sheltered bay. The water laps onto the sand and the quiet is like a balm to my soul.

"Why are we here?"

This way.

It takes an inordinate amount of effort to stand but I do, and Sahva leads me away from the beach, further into the lush plants that creep down to the edge of the sand, pushing his way through them, creating a dragon size path for me. And then, just behind a tumble-down pile of rocks, there's a small pool with steam rising from the surface.

I thought you might like to bathe.

The water looks like heaven. Now that there's a possibility of washing, the layer of dirt on my body itches my skin – in that moment – there's nothing I want more. I don't think about Sahva as I strip off my chest plate and clothes and slip into the pool. The emerald green water is deeper than I thought. Enough that I only have to bend a little to be submerged. A groan escapes me as the water warms the chills from my body. Wonderful and painful, all at the same time. Sahva rumbles, deep in his throat.

You sound like my little one when she was eating her favourite food.

I don't want to know what her favourite food might be, but talk of his 'little one' brings a question to my mouth that I'm not sure I want to let out. Do I want to do this; to know more about him? Hear the dragon's side of the story, as Bex hinted at? Ask the questions that might mean I see him as more than just my enemy? The enemy of my people . . . the people who just tried to kill me and would again if given half the chance, when they see the talon mark.

My hands swish through the water, and focusing on the ripples it creates, I take a deep breath. "You have a child?"

There. It's out. It sits in the air between us for a moment and he looks at me, blinking his eyes before he answers.

Yes. What you call children, we call whelps. We had three.

I can hear something in his voice. A sadness? An anger maybe? Whatever it is, he's trying not to show it. It makes me shiver, despite the warmth of the water, and the word is out of my mouth before I can stop it.

"Had?"

He turns his head away, as if he can't bear to look at me.

Before the war. Before the killing started.

It shames me that I've never given thought to the dragons, apart from the fact that they've hunted us for ten years. Never given thought to their lands or their families or their communities – that they might've even had communities. Or who they might have lost.

And then I remember who I've lost. Because of them. "Then why start it? Why kill? Why bring the war? Why take everything from us?"

My voice gets louder with each word, until I'm yelling at him. Screaming. Half out of the water in my rage.

We took nothing from you!

29

His words hit me like a slap, and his anger fuels my own.

"You took everything! Everything! My home, my safety, my future. My family. All but one and he's lost to me now. Because of this." I pull at my skin, stretching the mark. "And now you've taken everything else from me too. My freedom, my thoughts, my feelings. Even my actions aren't mine anymore if you don't want them to be. You can just command me! And I have to obey. Don't tell me you've taken nothing. You've taken every single thing that made me who I am!"

I'm panting by the end, not knowing if I want to rage more or sink into tears. So, I do neither. I just stand there, looking at him. Hating him.

His head swivels to mine and he draws back his mouth, showing his teeth in a way that makes me step back.

Do not talk to me about losing things important to you! You do not understand what that means. And yes, I marked you. Bonded with you. But that has given you more than you know. And I might be able to control your actions and your feelings if I choose to, but your thoughts are your own. I can never change those, as much as I would like to change all human thought. You are self-interested, irresponsible, greedy children who want what you want, no matter the consequences. His tail whips through the air and thumps into the ground like an exclamation point to his anger. *And this is why, in the years the war has raged around us, I*

30

have never bonded with a human, though it would have made me stronger. It was only because I was badly injured that I needed to do so. But it is the last thing I would ever have chosen. Humans are soft. Soft and sulky, like petulant whelps. Except our whelps grow whereas humans are always sulky. Always thinking about themselves and what they want and what they can take. Always taking. Taking. Taking. Enough!

I'm blasted by his words. Stunned by them. He doesn't give me time to respond before he turns, spreads his wings, and takes flight.

Leaving me here. Alone.

CHAPTER FIVE

I stay in the pool, waiting for him to return, fuming in the warm water like it's stewing my anger. When my fingers prune and it's clear he's not coming back – well, not anytime soon – I get out and scrub my clothes to some sort of cleanliness, muttering and beating them against the rock like I have a personal vendetta against the pieces of worn cloth. Wading back to the shore, I lay them out to dry in the warm sun, sitting on a rock in the warmth myself since there isn't anyone else around.

Once again, I have no idea where I am. On the coast, obviously. And I assume in the north because it's much warmer. And that's it. I was too cold and too sore to take much notice on the way here.

Not that Sahva will leave me in this place.

I can sense him although I'm certain he's not close. The connection between us is . . . stretched. In these last two days, I've become more aware of him, like an extension to my thoughts, but I can't hear what he's thinking unless he wants me to. I can feel his anger and sorrow like they're my own though.

It's not that which makes me certain he'll come back. It's how he's been the last two days. Thoughtful. Caring. Two words I never in my lifetime, thought I'd use about a dragon. Beasts. Killers. Monsters. They're the words we've been taught. They're the words we've experienced. And as much as I still want them to be true, they don't fit anymore. Like wet jigsaw puzzle pieces, swollen so they no longer join. I still know what the picture is but it's not perfect anymore – it's warped.

As the sun warms my skin, I think about what Sahva said before he left. That humans are soft and sulky. That we take what we want, only thinking of ourselves. And slivers of memories come back to me. My parents talking in worried, hushed tones when they thought we weren't listening. Speaking about the young King, who was only seventeen when the war started, and General Kaller, who'd been the general for the old King as well as the new. Whispering of agreements and peace treaties that had been broken.

I don't know how it all fits – the war, the dragons, our loss and theirs. I wonder what makes me so sure my loss is worse than Sahva's. And if maybe, to the people leading our country, we're all expendable victims in this war.

#

I'm dressed and watching the sun set when Sahva lands on the beach, swirling the sand with the wind from his wings so I have to cover my eyes and mouth. He says nothing, but drags a large branch from the edge of the forest, breaking it like it's a twig and breathing a fire to life in its embrace. I watch in silence as the flames die down and he places a large fish onto the coals. The smell of it makes my mouth water but still, I stay quiet.

Come. Eat.

The words are gruff but it isn't a command, so I choose to get off the rock and go over. The fish is delicious. Creamy and flaky and I've eaten a quarter of it before I realise.

"Do you want some?"

He snorts, and it puts the last of the fire out. *Cooked fish? No. I have already had my fill of fresh fish.*

He's silent again for a moment. *But I thank you for your consideration.*

I nod and pick the flesh of the fish off the bone. "I'm not sulky and soft," I say, looking up at him. "I've lost, just as you have."

He looks at me and then gives one of his slow blinks. The one I've come to associate with him thinking; taking in what I've said. Listening to me . . . *Yes.* His voice is soft in my head.

I move back to lean against a rock, bringing my legs up and hugging them to me.

What do you want to ask?

"How do you know I want to ask something?"

In the two days of our bond, since you have awoken, I have noticed that you bite your lip, just as you are doing now, when you have a question to ask.

So, it's not only me who's been paying attention then.

I push my legs out, digging up the sand with my toes, and sit up straighter. "I was twelve when the war started. And my parents . . . I lost them about six months after. My parents and my sisters,

34

all at the same time. My brother and I were the only survivors, and he was just five." I take a deep breath. It's been a long time since I've talked about this. Years. And yet, tears are threatening to rise and a hard lump forms in my throat. "We were so busy trying to survive, I don't really know much about the war. Why it started, what's happened. Except for bits of information I've overheard when searching for Gaiven in towns, I don't know much."

Twelve and five! You were just whelps.

I shrug. "It is what it is."

Sahva settles himself lower on the ground, folding his tail around him and tucking his wings closer against his body. *What do you know?*

"I know we were putting settlements along the border of our land and yours. And I know dragons came and burnt it all. The houses, the livestock. The people. Nothing was left except for three hunters who were coming back as it happened. They saw it all and escaped to tell the new King – his father had died only three months earlier – and General Kaller. And the war began, changing everything."

Yes, that did happen. I can hear the sigh in his thoughts; the regret, perhaps. *The villages were destroyed and everyone and everything in it. But there is more that happened before that. Dragons did not start the war.*

35

I go still, letting his words sink into my brain.

"What do you mean?"

He looks up at the stars, showing themselves now against the black sky, and is quiet for a long time. I find myself more patient than I've ever been before.

Tomorrow. I will show you tomorrow the catalyst for this war and answer any of your questions.

"But—"

No, Sage. Tomorrow. I am tired. It has been a big day, even with the extra strength our bond gives me.

And I can't argue with that but sleep doesn't come for a long time. I lay there, looking at the stars and listening to Sahva breathe, and wonder if I want to see what he's going to show me. Wonder if it will change my life more than it already has. And knowing I have to anyway.

CHAPTER SIX

In the morning, Sahva brings me another fish and I supplement it with some fruits at the edge of the forest. I've eaten better in the last few days than I have in the last two months. We're both quiet, listening to the soft wash of the waves onto the shore and the call of the birds in the trees. It's not uncomfortable sitting here with this enormous dragon. Just . . . sombre.

He rises in silence and I know it's time. I climb onto his back, still stiff from our ride over the two days and reluctant to face the mind-numbing chill again but I'm going anyway.

"How far do we need to go today?"

Not far. We are close to the border of our lands. This coast stretches across both countries but perhaps the swamp stops your people from populating it.

My heart sinks with the reminder that I will forever need to avoid people. After the reaction at the farm to my mark, I know Gaiven is lost to me, but still, it makes my chest tighten again, squeezing until I don't know if I can bear it.

What makes you sad?

I shake my head, not wanting to say it out loud, knowing the words will be a gateway for the tears.

Your brother.

I know Sahva can't read my thoughts – that he's said this

because he knows me. Understands me. It's scarier than him having access to my brain. How can he remain my enemy – this creature who's destroyed my life; destroyed me – when he knows me better than anyone has in a long, long time? When he appears to care for me? Worry that I'm sad?

He doesn't wait for an answer. He stretches out his wings and different shades of blues and blacks swirl together on his scales in the morning sun. Magnificent and dangerous, all at the same time.

The take-off is easier now I know what to expect and to see the world from above; the tops of trees rather than the underside, the birds launching themselves skyward, the rivers snaking their way onwards to the ocean, is like seeing the world from a different set of eyes. Proof that my whole life has changed irrevocably.

We are in dragon territory now.

Not that I can tell the difference. The same forests grow under us, the same birds fly from the trees. I wonder if we'll meet other dragons. And what they'll think of me. After all, Bex's dragon, Havil, hadn't made himself known to me. Perhaps they only tolerate the humans they've bonded with. I assume, with the mark, that I'll be safe. But maybe not. Maybe they'll feel the same way humans do. The thought makes my stomach twist and clench. I'm trusting Sahva to keep me safe. And I'm not certain he will, when faced with his own kind. He'd said he'd resisted bonding with a human until he'd had no other choice. Maybe all dragons feel that way . . .

I had not realised that humans suffer so many changing emotions.

There is a gruffness to his voice. Perhaps even a sorrow. Well, he can suffer through them with me. I don't care. He chose to mark me. He'll have to deal with feeling it too.

There are spaces within the green; places where rocks have been piled on top of and around each other, like a rocky nest. And I wonder if that's what it is. Is there where dragon children are raised? And yet, it's curious that none of them are in use if that's what they're for. Although we're close to the border so perhaps all the whelps have been moved further away.

With a savage suddenness that makes my heart stutter, a blood red dragon angles up to block our flight. It's smaller than Sahva but no less fearsome and I duck down lower on Sahva's back, although there's no chance of hiding myself.

The dragon flies in tighter circles around us, forcing Sahva lower and lower until he has no choice but to land. Frustration rather than anger radiates off him, and I'm somewhat reassured by this, but choose not to slide off his back when he touches down.

You are safe, Sahva says.

The other dragon lands in front of us, its face held low, close to Sahva's, and wings still unfolded, as if to make itself bigger.

Cadex, Sahva says, his voice echoing differently in my head as he includes me in his conversation with this new dragon.

Sahva. The dragon hisses his name. *How dare you bring one of them onto our lands. Her kind should be all dead, not on the back of a dragon, protected like a pet!*

We are bonded. She is not a threat.

They are all a threat. Their greed and their duplicity means they cannot be trusted! How could you bond with one? You, who have lost so much and swore to never create that connection?

Cadex lurches forward, teeth bared as if she'd love nothing more than to close them around my neck.

Stop, Cadex. Sahva's voice holds a strong command and she backs away again. *There has been enough killing; enough hatred. I am taking her to see.*

For a long moment, there's silence from the dragon and then, her wings sag. *Why?*

Because she has lost too. As much as we have.

Their King has not lost. Nor their General. Her wings are up again.

No. But Sage is not them. She has lost. And she should understand.

The dragon turns her head away, looking out across the rocks to the trees.

She should not stay here, she says finally.

No, Sahva agrees. *I will show her so that she understands, and then we shall leave.*

There's a part of me that wants to ask why we can't stay; that rages because Sahva and I aren't welcome anywhere. That we're not safe anywhere.

But it's enough that the dragon lets us leave again, watching us until I can no longer see her.

Why is she so angry at my being here? I ask.

She has lost, too. Those words explain everything.

Up ahead, I see a change to the green of the forest. It's only as we got closer that I realise it's a dead zone – an enormous swathe of orange earth laid bare like someone has taken a huge knife and slashed a wound open, leaving it to fester. Sahva tucks his wings, diving us down, closer and closer until I'm sure we're going to smash into the ground, only at the last minute opening his wings and setting us on the earth.

My heart is pounding in my chest, stomach rolling, and I'm ready to berate him – tell him not to do that again – but as I slide off into the orange dust, his agitation is clear; in the twitching of his tail, the drawing back of his neck, as if at any moment he's going to produce flame. "Where are we?"

We are where the war started.

I look around me, eyes narrowed, unsure what his words mean. "But we're on dragon land."

Yes.

His tail whips in the air, coming down with a loud thwack that echoes over the barren land. *Come.*

And even though I don't want to, I follow him up to the ridge of the small rise he's landed us on. Below us, strange white rocks litter the landscape, and a river runs red and brown, like blood in the orange wound. It's not a good place – not a healthy place – and, all of a sudden, I want nothing more than to climb back on Sahva and fly away. Get away from this dead space.

The river was called Harttron. Life Giver.

I look up at him and then back at the river. *Was.* It's a word that speaks volumes. "What happened?"

Your general, he spits the word, *ordered it to be poisoned. Your King was young and weak and perhaps did not know what the General had done. But it makes no difference. It still happened and we could not let it go unpunished.*

I frown. That makes no sense. It's on dragon land. And while I might not know much about the war, I know about the treaty between humans and dragons. The one that had been in existence for hundreds of years. The one that had always kept a fragile peace between us, until ten years ago. "I don't understand. Why would he do that?"

Sahva swings his head down so quickly I take a step back. His golden eyes are narrowed as he looks at me.

Why do you think? Greed. Power. Humans think they can take

42

whatever they want without thought of others. Without thought of the sorrow or hurt they cause, especially if the others are not human.

My mouth is dry and I swallow hard, and then do it again. Buying myself time before I respond.

"But that doesn't make any sense. What about the treaty? The one we've had for centuries? It kept us *all* safe."

A treaty only works if both sides abide by it. The power of the dragons and the magic we possess has always helped keep man's greed in check. Before. And then this happened.

I shake my head, still not able to comprehend what he's saying. Not when it's so different to the story I've heard, over and over, in the last ten years. "But why would the General poison it? What good would it do? What's the point?"

I'm repeating myself but I can't sort it in my head. There was no point in anyone – a general, no less, doing what Sahva says he'd done. It is such an idiotic decision! Why break the treaty, incite war, create so much death and poverty in our own country; why do all of that when there was no way we could use this land now? No way this benefitted the kingdom at all.

An angry rumble comes from him, spreading over the land like a precursor to a storm. *Look closely at the ground. We do not ask for comprehension. We see that death that has been wrought and seek vengeance.*

I look again. Really look. It isn't rocks spread over the orange dirt. The white things are bones. Thousands of bones, covering the earth like a morbid quilt. I cover my mouth, nausea rising up in me, overwhelming me.

The bones of my kin. Hundreds of them. Killed before we realised the water was poisoned. That our life-giver had been made our life-taker.

My hand covers my mouth, unable to comprehend the amount of death before me, all in one place.

We were too strong – too much of a threat – to break the treaty. So, he reduced us. Tried to weaken us. But we have shown him. We have proven we are not weak, no matter how much he tries to destroy us.

I can't keep it in any longer. I turn, bringing up the contents of my stomach on the dry ground, heaving until there's nothing left. Sahva is silent beside me. My head reels from the thoughts racing through it, trying to find purchase. None of this makes sense to me.

"How could he do that? All this death. All our deaths. My family. So many dragons. So many people. Why?" But I know, as the words leave my mouth, there's no answer he can give.

Sahva turned back to the bones around us. *Your family. And mine. My mate is here. And my three whelps. It was only because I was hunting for food that I survived.*

For a moment, he's silent again. *Sometimes I wish I had not.*

These words echo the ones I've said in my head since finding my family dead and I reach out, touching his leg. His scales quiver beneath my hand and in that moment, I understand that loss is loss. The other details mean nothing.

And now you understand why we fight. Why we kill. Why we defend what little we have left to us.

And I do. Even if I wish, beyond anything, that I didn't need to. That all of this had never happened. That our General and perhaps our King – our so-called protectors – had kept their word. But wishes are for children and foolish adults, as my father used to say, and I'd had to stop being foolish a long time ago.

The question that has plagued me for days comes back. One I have to ask, yet dread having answered.

Ask. Savha says. Of course, he senses it.

"When I saw you that morning, when we were bound . . . why were you there? On the human side of the border?"

He sighs and it ruffles my hair. *Your soldiers had killed two of our whelps who had crept closer to the border, eager to see the conflict without really understanding the war. The violence. The hatred. Two gone when we have so few still to protect. They were too young to produce flame, compel minds. They had no defence except physical and were easily overwhelmed by the army. I could not let that go unpunished.*

Whelps. Children. All dead because of an abhorrent, terrible, *evil* decision the General made. It overwhelms me, like a heavy blanket, holding me down.

Come. We will leave. There is only death and sorrow here now.

I nod wearily and climb his leg, settling once again in the groove on his back, leaning my forehead for a moment, against the scales on his neck. "Where are we going?"

To make at least one thing right.

But I am too weary; too heartsore, to ask what he means.

#

He flies low over the ocean, the warm sea breeze keeping the numbing cold at bay. We've been flying for hours and my stomach is grumbling, never satisfied, as if it once again expects food every day.

Sahva must feel it too, because – without warning – he dips until we are so close to the waves, I can almost touch them. And with a spray of water, he reaches down and spears a fish, making it look easy. I don't try to stop the small laugh that escapes my lips. It feels nice after the heavy sorrow.

"Show off," I say. His laughter rumbles at my words, and then we're aiming for a small island, its sand a bright white in the noon day sun, a light sprinkling of green covering the interior.

I drag branches over, although my effort is embarrassingly insignificant to the amount Sahva brings. He ignites the wood and leaves me to cook the fish, wrapped in leaves, while he goes to hunt for himself. I'm pulling the last of the flesh from the bones when he returns.

"Where are we?" It's a constant question on my lips but it needs to be when we can cover so much ground and I'm still not used to getting my bearings from the air.

I don't know what humans call this island but it is north of the tip of your land. The tip where you keep all the boats.

Axiam? We're near Axiam! I can hardly breathe. I don't know if it's excitement or fear. I'm a ball of conflicting emotion. "Why? Why are we here?"

To make one thing right. Your brother is near this place? That's why you were coming here, was it not?

"Yes." The word isn't much more than a whisper.

He brings his head close to mine. *What is wrong? I thought you wanted to find your brother. Is this not what you were planning, before I marked you with our bond?*

"Yes. Of course. But . . ."

But?

"What if he won't accept me with . . . with this?" My hand goes to the mark.

It is up to you if you think it is worth the risk.

I don't know if it's that easy. I want to see him. More than anything in the world, I want to see him and know he's okay. What if he's not there though? What if this was all for nothing and I have no way of getting more information about where he is now? He'd be lost to me forever.

Or what if he sees me and wants to kill me? Gods, I don't know that I could cope with the anguish of that. Would I let him? Would I want him to live with that for the rest of his life? My stomach curls and twists up on itself, threatening to bring back up the fish I've just eaten.

But I keep my doubts to myself. If Sahva finds my emotions confusing, then dragons and humans must think very differently and I'm not in the headspace where I can take the time to explain it to him.

He does one of his long, slow blinks.

I am sorry that having to do what I did makes you different. That it makes others of your kind distrust you. If I could change how they react, then I would. He pauses. *But I would not unmark you.*

Those words don't anger me like they would've yesterday, before our trip to the dragon lands. And I'm not sure why, except my view of him has changed. I wonder though, why he would say that . . . if it's for the same reasons?

I toy with the buckle on my chest plate. "Why? You didn't want this anymore than I did."

He drags a paw through the sand, leaving groves with his talons. *I feel as if I know you better than any other living thing.*

And while that is disconcerting – you are a human and you have so many emotions – it is also comforting. A closeness I have not experienced for a long time. And I would not want to lose that. It has become . . . you have become . . . important to me.

And as much as I hate to admit it, I feel the same. Bex was right.

CHAPTER SEVEN

We land at a rocky outcrop at the bottom of a steep mountain, the land not suitable for crops so it's uninhabited, although it's only a half day walk to Axiam from here. Deserted and far enough away so that no one will notice Sahva. Hopefully.

"Will you be okay?" I ask.

It's a strange feeling to be worried about someone other than my brother. Having to move often, following every lead, I've been separate from people for such a long time; too itinerant to form new relationships, that it feels like retraining a muscle that hasn't been used for years.

He snorts and the dust in front of him stirs and settles . . . the dragon equivalent of an eye roll.

Worry more about yourself. I do not want to have to fly into a settlement to rescue you. He pauses, swinging his head closer to me. *But I will, if you need me.*

I hesitate, wondering if I can ask what I want of him . . . whether I *should* ask it of him.

What is it?

I sigh. There's to be no secrets in my life anymore, it would seem. From Sahva, anyway, unless I get better at hiding my emotions.

"I'd like to bring my brother back to meet you. Even if he

chooses to stay here, in his life at Axiam, I'd like him to see you. To know I'm okay and that you're . . . kind to me."

Sahva does his slow blink and I wait. *He may not understand, no matter how much you explain it to him. If he was the bonded one, would you believe him or would you think his dragon was making him say it? Would you still fight to free him?*

"I know," I say, kicking my boot against the dirt. "That's why I'd like to bring him back, so he can see how good you are. That you're not the monster King Luka and General Kaller tells us dragons are."

He inclines his head, and a sense of pleasure comes through our link at my words. *I am happy to meet your brother if you wish it.*

I nod, offering a small smile before turning in the direction of the city. The land I walk is littered with sparsely vegetated dirt and rocks. There are no cornbows here, but that's not important anymore. I tuck my head against the cold sea breeze, which bites into my skin, numbing it as it swirls around me

As I get closer to the outskirts of Axiam, I wipe dirt over my cheek. It doesn't cover it but should offer some camouflage. Drawing my hair over my shoulder, I braid it in a way that brings it forward and hides the mark in shadows. Enough that it won't be noticed at first glance anyway.

The outskirts of the city are busy with activity as I make my way through the gates. People going about their work, shopping, tending to horses, talking in groups, moving down to the marina. Busy people are good. Busy people don't care about a lone girl in old clothes who appears to be of no threat, and not worth robbing or taking notice of. I'm invisible to them. I make sure to keep my eyes down however, just in case. There's no point in attracting any attention or interest if I can help it.

I make my way to the barracks on the eastern wall. The last information I had was that Gaiven was with the surgeon to the army, doing the role of assistant with a view to becoming a medical apprentice. It's a good opportunity – something that, as likely as not, wouldn't have been available to him before the war. And if he chooses to stay, I don't want to jeopardise that for him by creating a disturbance. I don't want him to be known as the brother of a talon marked traitor.

I need to see him though. It feels selfish but I need to see that he is okay; not being mistreated or taken advantage of. I want to see that he's happy. And I need him to know I'm still alive. I don't know if that's for me or him but it doesn't matter. It has to happen.

The number of soldiers at the barracks takes my breath away. There are hundreds of them. It's not what I anticipated. I expected them to be off fighting, closer to the border, with only the sick and injured under the care of the surgeon here, but they're doing exercises, practicing with weapons, standing and chatting.

Soldiers are everywhere I look.

And I'm a talon marked girl.

So close. I am so close to finding him and yet the ocean of men in front of me is like a physical barrier. My stomach knots, and then knots some more until I'm sure it's about to explode with tension.

I need to find him. I need to!

"Can I help you, Miss?"

My eyes flick up. A young officer stands in front of me, his forehead crinkled as he watches me. Turning slightly so my mark is further from him, I pray he can't see how nervous I am.

"I'm looking for Gaiven. Gaiven Berryman. He helps the surgeon."

He smiles. "Gaiv. Sure. That white building over there."

He points to a building at the edge of the barracks and for once, it's as if luck has smiled on me. It's away from the main centre, and more importantly, away from the men.

"Thanks." I turn to go.

"Are you family?"

That stops me. I look at him again, body on alert. "What makes you say that?"

He shrugs. "Gaiv's always talking about his sister. How much she looked after him. How brave she was. And how he lost her."

His face softens. "He's missed you."

I nod and turn before he can see the tears in my eyes. He's missed me? I'd talked myself into thinking he'd forgotten all about me.

The walk to the white building takes forever and, conscious of the fact that the soldier may still be watching me, I keep my head down and walk as fast as I can. It takes a moment for my eyes to adjust to the dim light in the room. It's empty, except for the young man in the corner at the desk. It takes me a few precious seconds to work out that the man sitting there writing is Gaiven!

I watch him, my eyes hungry for every detail. He's taller than when I last saw him – even sitting down I can tell that. And he looks more like our father, now that his jaw and shoulders have filled out. His hair is all our mother's though, the exact same golden shade that my father used to say was like ripened wheat in the sunlight. He even has the same cowlick at the front. I move without thinking, wanting to be able to see more of him and he looks up.

His eyes widen as he recognises me and then he is up, knocking the table over in his haste. Having him in my arms fills my heart with a happiness I can't ever remember feeling. He wraps his arms around me, taller than me now, and it's a hug that's familiar and not, both at the same time.

"Oh my God, Sage. Sage, Sage, Sage."

And then he's sobbing in my arms and I'm crying too and we're a mix of tears and laughter and sobs and hugs. He steps back finally, although his hand is still on my arm, as if he's unwilling to lose contact.

"How did you find me?"

I touch his face. "I never stopped looking, asking. Never. It's taken me longer than I thought. I'm sorry."

He shakes his head. "Don't say that. You don't have anything to be sorry for." He wipes his eyes with one hand, rough and impatient. "I heard a noise, that morning. And I was an idiot. I should've woken you first but, I went to check it out." He let out a sigh. "It was a group of soldiers. They were drunk and they grabbed me, telling me I was old enough to be a part of the army. And I didn't want them to know you were there. I didn't know what they'd do if they found you. I needed to protect you."

I hug him to me again, my heart aching with the responsibility he'd felt to protect me and he lays his head on my shoulder, continuing his story.

"I thought if I just went with them, drew them away, then I'd find a chance to escape and get back to you. But I couldn't, Sage. I couldn't get away from them."

I stroke his back. "Shh, it's okay. We found each other again, that's all that matters."

His arms tighten around me for a moment and then he pulls

back.

The inhale of breath tells me he's seen it. The talon mark. And I brace myself. Harden my heart. If I have to leave now, I know he's okay. And he knows I'm alive. That's all that matters. It is. It is . . .

"Oh my God, Sage! Is that . . ?"

I nod. Silent.

"What happened?"

He hasn't moved away but there's a sudden barrier between us. I tell him anyway. He deserves to know, so he won't have to keep wondering when I'm not here to answer.

The tale is quicker than I thought it would be, but then it has only been four days, as strange as that sounds. Not the lifetime I'm sure it's taken. Such a huge change for me and yet, it can all be summed up in a few minutes.

I don't tell him about our visit to the dragons lands though. Despite the fact that he has thrived without me, I still feel the need to protect him. While I'm proud how well he's done on his own, and honest enough to admit it's tinged with some sorrow that I'm no longer needed, I'm not sure what his reaction will be now he's entrenched in the army. And I don't want to push him too much.

He doesn't say a word while I talk and, at the end, he's still silent. I wait for him to take it all in, make sense of it. Finally, a furrow between his eyes, he brings his hand up, hovering near my cheek.

"Can I?"

I nod. His touch overwhelms me and I shut my eyes, only to open them again when I feel his hand gone.

"Can you run away? Maybe we can help you? The soldiers? Or maybe Dr Dolp can cut it out? Get rid of it."

I shake my head. "There's nothing they can do, Gaiv. I'm marked. Bonded. And it's okay. Truly it is. Sahva is good. Kind even."

Four days ago, I would've never believed those words would come from my mouth; would've slapped someone for suggesting it. And yet, they're the truth. They make his frown deepen though.

"Sahva?"

"The dragon who marked me."

"You know his name? How can he be good? What do you mean? They kill us! They killed Mum and Dad and Avrim and Kate! And now he has you; he's taken you from me. I'll kill him! I will. I'll save you. I promise."

"Shh, shh." I pull him to me, cupping his face in my hands, frightened his anger will lead others to us to see what's wrong. "Gaiven, you need to listen to me."

"I'll protect you, Sagey, let me protect you." It's his pet name for me, said in a crumbled voice, and it undoes me.

"Gaiv. Oh Gaiv. You can't. You can't. If they see it, they'll kill me. You know that. You know that's what happens to talon marked. But I'm okay. I just needed to know you were okay too."

It's on the tip of my tongue to tell him about what Sahva showed me this morning so he understands, even though I'd been resolute in keeping it from him. I want to tell him about the war and how it started so he can understand how a dragon can be good, but I can't put that on him. I can't give him that responsibility and leave. He's only fifteen. They'll kill him to keep him quiet if they have to. What's one more death to them, amongst so many?

And while it'd sounded like a good idea when I talked to Sahva, I know now that taking him to meet the dragon won't fix things. Won't change things in his mind. I count myself lucky instead, that he didn't pull away in disgust when he first saw the mark. Or out me as a traitor. That is enough. I can take the moment with me and be happy.

"I have to go before anyone sees me and notices the mark. Okay? I love you. I love you. Be happy."

And I'm pulling away from him, my head telling me I need to leave even if my heart is fighting it.

"No, no. Sage. Stay. Stay with me. Please!"

Sage! They are here! They have found us! They are coming for you. Hide!

Sahva! In danger, only because I asked him to stay.

No!

And I run.

Outside is organised chaos as soldiers form into groups, weapons – so many weapons – ready to kill a dragon. Like they have before. Like they will again. I don't know what I think I'm going to do but I have to get to Sahva.

Gaiven catches me, quicker than he used to be because of his extra height, pulling on my hand. "Sage!"

"Gaiven. Let me go. I have to go to him. They're going to kill me. Do you understand? They'll kill him and they'll kill me!"

"No. No, they won't. I'll protect you. And they can kill him and then you'll be free."

I won't be though. I'm marked and will always be marked. An outsider now, even if my dragon is dead. Not that that's not important anymore. I can't let them hurt Sahva. That's what *is* important. Even if he commanded me to go, I think, on this, I'd be able to resist. My need to protect him is as strong as his need to protect me.

People are turning to look at us now. The strange girl and the young boy they all know, holding on to her. And it only takes a minute, like I knew it would, before it starts.

"The mark!"

"She's talon marked!"

"Dragon traitor!"

I pull at Gaiven's hand.

"Let me go, Gaiv. You have to go. Be safe."

I wrench my arm from his grip and run. It takes a moment for the soldiers to make chase but I'm small, quick and nimble and not weighed down by weapons. I run through the streets that I'd tried so hard to be inconspicuous in less than an hour ago, towards the still open gate. I'm no longer trying to hide. There's no time. Instead, I dodge people before they realise what's happening, despite the soldiers yelling for someone to stop me as they run in my wake.

They're setting up the ballista positioned around the walls; loading them with the bolts that can take down a dragon easily if the accuracy is good. Panic makes me run faster, my breath coming from me in gasps.

And then I'm through the gates and free of the city walls. Free. Although who knows for how long.

A shadow falls over me. Sahva. Having flown from the mountain side where he'd been waiting. Here to protect me and all I can picture is a bolt tearing through his scales.

"Go. Go!" I yell, but either he doesn't hear or he ignores me like I ignored him.

He lands, thudding down in his haste, so different from his usual, graceful landing, and I run to him.

But the soldiers have caught up to me, and as I reach Sahva, one grabs my arm, yanking me to his chest and wrapping his arm around my neck. I struggle, lashing out with my fists, my legs, but he's so much stronger than I am and the tightening arm around my neck makes it hard to breathe. Sahva roars, whipping his tail around into the soldier's back, knocking us both to the ground. The soldier's weight on my body stuns me for a second but the thought that he might grab me again is enough to make me buck and kick until he's off me. He doesn't move and I don't stop to see if he's dead.

Hurry! Hurry!

I climb onto Sahva's leg, ready to hoist myself onto his back, and look over my shoulder. The rest of the soldiers are almost on us. And Gaiven is with them. Sahva takes a breath and I know – without knowing how – that he's about to breathe fire. Burn them all before they can hurt us. Protecting without thought.

"No. No!" I scream so loud my throat hurts. "That's my brother!"

He pulls back, stopping himself, and then they are there, and a soldier lunges at Sahva with his backstaff, going for his chest.

I leap from Sahva's leg, throwing myself at the soldier, and the blade bites into my side between the joins of my chest plate, cutting deep into my flesh. The pain comes seconds later as I hit the ground.

"Go, Sahva. Get away!" I try to yell the words but it takes so much effort, I'm not even sure he'll hear. He stands over me, biting into flesh, tearing with talons, using his tail like a whip. Protecting me from the soldiers that are still coming from the gates and I know that this is it. They'll overwhelm him, kill us. And all I can think is that I don't want Gaiv to have to see it happen.

My blood is seeping into the dry ground and my energy going with it. Maybe they won't have to kill me. Maybe I'll already be dead. And that will save Gaiv having to witness my execution.

I take a deep breath. In and out. And then there's nothing but blackness.

CHAPTER EIGHT

There's a sweet smell to the air when I open my eyes. It's dark again. Night. And then I remember what happened.

I lurch up, the pain only a vague memory, my hand going to my side. My chest plate has been removed and my shirt is little more than a shredded rag. The light from the fire illuminates the new pink scar on my ribs, and I trace its raised length with my finger. Not a dream then, not that I thought it was. The memory of the pain is still too fresh. I should be dead.

Sahva is lying next to me, eyes closed.

It is good to see you awake, Sage. I have been worried that the shock might have been too much for you.

"How long have I been unconscious?"

A day.

I frown and touch my side again. The scar *isn't* a day old. "It can't be. Only a day?"

Did you not believe me when I said the bond gives you strength as well? You share the protection of my magic. The only way you can be killed is by a blow to your heart or to remove your head. Even if I die, you will live for a long time. As long as a dragon. Many hundreds of years.

Hundreds of years! My brain is stunned into silence. I don't know how to answer or make any sense of it. Hundreds of years

. . . I shake my head. This is something to deal with later. Not now.

"Are you okay? Did they hurt you?"

He opens his eyes. *I have healed from the minor scratches they inflicted on me and am fine. I am a bit tired from the healing I had to do on you, but fine. When you jumped in front of the blade, you saved my life. Why did you do that? You did not fully understand at the time that it was harder for you to die and yet, you were willing to sacrifice yourself for me. Why?*

I shrug and fiddle with the shredded ends of my shirt. The relief that he's okay swamps my body, the same sensation as seeing that Gaiv was happy and safe after so long. "You saved my brother because I asked you to, even though it put you in danger. And you're my . . . friend. I didn't want you to die. I couldn't let them kill you."

He blinks, the rest of his body perfectly still. And this time, he's silent as if he has to think about my words before he responds.

I make myself more comfortable, curling my legs under me and pulling the remains of my shirt tighter around my body. Another set of clothes has become a necessity, rather than an unmet want, and I think about where I might be able to get some. Another reason to regret my unplanned flight from the ravine that first night, leaving my backpack and all my spare clothes

And still, he is silent and I let him have the space.

I stare at the stars for hours, letting the immenseness of the sky still my thoughts. Finally, I sigh. "Now what?"

He rustles his wings, as if he's coming back from his thoughts too, and then brings his head closer to me. *I have thought hard while you have been recuperating and my mind continues to settle on one thought only. And that is that there has been enough killing, from both sides. Enough loss and upheaval. Now, we must stop this war.*

His words shock a startled laugh out of me. And then I realise he's serious and I sit forward, folding my arms around my knees. "And how do we do that? The war's been going for ten years. How do we convince either the dragons or humans to give in, because neither are going to want to? And *you're* not that scary on your own."

He rumbles, low in his stomach. The noise that sounds like a laugh. *We have someone we need to see, friend.*

#

The mountain air is bitingly cold and I'm thankful that we took time to steal new clothes and a chest plate before we came here. This new chest plate is stiffer, especially around the buckles, but I'm glad of its extra warmth as the mountains below us are dusted with snow.

Guilt stabs my stomach when I think about the family we took the clothes from. I would've left money for them if I had any.

Perhaps when all of this is over, I can go back, if I get the chance to.

We'd flown through the day and night and into the next day over the dragon lands and then headed out over the southern ocean; far out across the sea to avoid being seen by other humans, to the spine of mountains that ran along the southern end of Varunah. We'd seen other dragons but none of them had approached us and, in the far distance, the fires and camps of the army illuminated the darkness, as they waited for a chance to take down another dragon.

The cottage that Sahva is flying us to is set halfway up the mountain, clinging to the side like lichen on a tree trunk and surrounded by snow-covered fir trees. It's a picturesque vista, untouched by the war that has raged for so many years. I don't know how that's possible. Except that this is where Sahva believes the Sorceress has hidden for the last ten years.

I'd been stunned into silence when he told me who we were seeking. The Sorceress – our magic user who'd been condemned by the General and the King at the beginning of the war as a dragon traitor, even without a talon mark. The wanted posters with her image, spread across the land, have a bounty that would allow me to buy four farms if I wanted and yet, no one has seen her. Not in the whole ten years.

I'm surprised that she hadn't fled to the dragon side of the border, given that she'd been accused of siding with the dragons in the war but I can't pretend to know the magic user's reasoning for staying on Varunah.

You do not have to be nervous. I will protect you.

I snort, not that he can hear me through the layers of fabric wrapped around my nose and mouth. While dragons have their own powers, it's nothing to the power of the Sorceress. She's the reason our country had been so strong for such a long time and the school history books said she'd lived for centuries, serving a succession of kings.

There's been constant rumours of her death after her defection to the dragons was made public, despite the fact that new wanted posters are being put up all the time. Not that I've paid that much attention to the talk. My focus had been on keeping myself and my brother alive; there had been little time to worry about the machinations of people so far above my rank in the community.

A slab of black and grey flint rock, sitting further up the mountain and uncovered by snow, stands out against the white, and it's here that Sahva lands.

It would be rude to land in her front yard unannounced, he says as I slide from his back.

While I'm not looking forward to trekking through the snow in boots that are long past weatherproof, it's definitely preferable to angering someone with that level of magic.

By the time we've trekked and slid in equal measure down the side of the mountain, my feet are wet and numb from the cold and I'm glad when we make it to the cabin. It's small – only one or two rooms from the look of the outside – and is built from rough-hewn logs slotted together. Different to what I would've expected for a sorceress like Talme. Much less . . . grand.

There's a man watching us walk through the snow. He's big – tall and wide with muscles that are evident, even standing still. It's obvious he makes use of the axe he's cradling in his arms and while his dark beard does a good job of hiding his expression, his stance isn't at all welcoming.

My heart is telling me to just continue walking down the hill while I still can, thumping out a warning I'm doing my best to ignore. I rest my hand on Sahva's side and it settles me a little.

The man's eyebrows rise at my movement and I'm not sure what he reads from it, but he shifts, lowering the axe to the ground and leaning on it. He inclines his head towards us. "Dragon. Girl."

I try not to bristle at the term. It's been a long time since I've felt young enough to be called a girl, but it's not important. Not enough that I want to pick a fight with this man over it.

Sorceress Talme. Sahva's low growl punctuates his greeting. His voice once more has an echo to it as he projects it out to both the man and me.

I frown, confused at his words. The wanted pictures of Talme

68

show a petite woman; the complete opposite of the man standing in front of us.

The man smiles. It doesn't help my confusion. But then he brings his hand up, as if he's gripping the air in front of his face before pulling it away. And in front of us now is the petite woman from the pictures, smaller than Gaiven was at ten, with severely cut dark hair, dressed in a heavy, green, brocade gown. It's a dress that belongs to the women of the court. She looks to be fifty at the most, with only thin lines marring the skin around her eyes and mouth, despite the fact that she's centuries old.

"I should've known a dragon would see through the glamour straight away," she says, smoothing her hands down her dress. "It's been too long since I've been around your kind."

Ten years at least.

There's something in the way Sahva says that – something accusing, that makes me glance between the woman and dragon. Is it because she *has* stayed away during the war, holed up here in the mountains? That she hasn't helped the dragons as she's been accused of? When he said we were to come here to find the Sorceress, I thought it was to ask for her help but now I'm not sure.

The smile slides from her face and she sighs. "Yes. Ten years, as you say. Well, I suppose you'd better come in out of the cold."

I look from her to Sahva to the cabin and back again. Being

alone must've warped her brain. There's no way a dragon will fit into the small cottage. They both move forward though, leaving me standing there, and unless I want to shiver in the snow by myself, I have no choice but to follow.

It's when I move closer to the cottage that it happens; a feeling like nothing I've experienced before, as if tiny, ice-cold needles are pressing into every part of my skin. My gasp has Sahva and Talme turning back to look at me.

"Keep coming," Talme says, turning away and continuing to walk, not at all concerned that my skin now feels like it's on fire. "It's the glamour. The feeling will stop when you take a few more steps."

I don't know if I believe her and for a second, think about stepping back. But I've never been a coward and am not about to start now. I step forward, like I'm pushing through a physical barrier, jaw clenched, and Sahva grumbles a laugh.

I forgot it would affect you as a human. Dragons are not influenced by glamours.

I want to make a sarcastic remark but instead, am stunned speechless by what's in front of me. Gone is the tiny, roughly-hewn cabin and in its place is an elegant, low set home, built of dark, sleek wood, spreading out over the flattened earth. The three sides of the building wrap around a central area, and a large fire pit in the middle warms the air. The roof over the top of this space is high enough for Sahva to fit under and he settles himself near the fire with a contented sigh.

Talme sits with a grace I don't think I could ever emulate, on an intricately carved seat made from the same dark wood as the house, and looks over to me. "Stop gawping, girl, and come sit."

I hurry over. The warmth of the fire makes me shiver and I sit on the floor next to Sahva, my body defrosting.

Remove your boots before your toes fall off. She will not be offended. His voice is echoing again and I glance over at the Sorceress, unsure, but she nods at me.

"Do as your dragon says. It makes no difference to me and I would prefer to not have to cure frostbite today."

I don't wait to be told again, dragging my boots off and putting them close to the fire to dry. My toes tingle painfully as they warm but it's a feeling I'm thankful for.

"Now tell me, dragon, why you've decided to come here today, after so long?" Talme sits like a queen in her chair, chin up, shoulders squared, as she watches us. It's as if she's waiting to be attacked by our words although there's nothing I want to say to her. And yet we wait and wait for Sahva to answer her question. The tension created by his silence makes my shoulders tight.

You have chosen, Sorceress, to be separate from your country for a long time, he says finally, just as I'm ready to say something . . . anything! . . . to break the silence.

Talme doesn't comment on that. Instead, she repeats her question. "Why are you here, dragon?"

Sahva's tail twitches, like that of the cat we'd had as a child, and his agitation radiates through our bond. *You need to correct the atrocity you caused. Take responsibility for your actions and stop the constant killing that is being perpetuated by both sides. Restore peace.*

I have no idea what he's talking about but it's evident that Talme does; she leans forward in her seat, her movements jerky, her words hissing out at Sahva.

"I did *not* cause the terrible situation that happened. I would never – *never* – have allowed that! And you know it. You know the relationship I had with the dragons. Why would I do that when our magics are so closely linked?"

And yet, despite your fine words, your magic was used!

"Without my knowledge!" Talme is standing now. She seems to have grown taller in the last few seconds but maybe it's the power that's rolling off her in waves. Her green eyes are glowing and I'm just as terrified as when I first saw Sahva in the clearing.

There's no doubt in my mind that if she wanted to kill me right now, she could do so. I push my hands down on the ground beside me, ready to take flight, even though there'd be no possibility of outrunning her magic.

Sahva's neck is extended, towering over Talme, but in that

moment, he lowers his head and huffs, and some of the emotion drains from him. *Be calm, Sorceress. I did not want to believe you would deliberately be a part of the death of so many of my kind but I had to be sure. I can feel the truth in the words you speak.*

Talme's magic is still crackling in the air as she stares at him, but after several minutes, she sits again, taking a moment to arrange her dress around her until it's perfect.

"Wait. Was your magic used to poison the river and kill the dragons? Did you start the war? But you've been sentenced to death for *helping* the dragons!" There's a part of me that can't believe I'm brave enough, or maybe stupid enough, to ask the questions but it's impossible to stop the words from leaving my mouth.

Talme's eyes narrow as she looks at me. "No, chit. I did not start the war. Do not talk of things that are beyond your understanding."

My hands clench at the rudeness of her words – at her dismissal – but I don't have a death wish, so I stay silent.

Talme's magic was used. Sahva's calmness comes through our link – not as if he's trying to influence my emotions but as if he's supporting me. *But it appears she was not aware that this was what it would be used for. She had been part of our community at times in the two hundred years before the atrocity and had been accepted by us. It seemed a traitorous thing to do from someone*

73

who had never shown that part of herself before.

I look back at the Sorceress and her face is blank, as if Sahva's words have no effect on her. I remember the bones, though, spread over the ground. The thousands of dragons that died. Sahva's family . . .

"But why didn't you fix things then?" My frustration, my anger, colours my words but in this moment, I don't care. All of this . . . all the lives lost, both human and dragon – what's the point to it? What are we fighting for, except the power and greed that Sahva's talked about? "If you knew your magic had been used, why didn't you make things right? Fix the river? Punish the person responsible? Try to end the war before it even started?"

Talme's harsh laugh fills the air. "It's so easy when you say it like that, isn't it? It must be nice to still be a child without hundreds of years of politics to have to navigate."

My scowl deepens. "I'm not a child! I've lost my family. As has Sahva. This war is all I remember. It hasn't allowed me to be a child, so don't treat me like one. You have no right!"

Talme's eyes flick over me, before going to Sahva, and then coming back to rest on my face. "No." Her body sags and she runs her hands over her dress until the material on her lap is once again smooth. "No. Forgive me. It has been so long since I've spoken to anyone apart from my apprentice, I sometimes forget the continued pain that consumes our world."

Sage has asked an important question, however. Why did you choose to withdraw? Why not help create balance in our worlds again before we had to experience so many years of violence and hatred? Was the threat of death enough to keep you away?

The sorceress grips her hands in front of her, as if trying to hold herself together. "I couldn't do anything in the beginning. So many dragons were already dead, and so quickly, that it had all happened before I was aware of it. But the guilt I felt; the horror when I realised it was *my* magic they'd used to create this genocide paralysed me with grief and guilt." Her voice is strained and she stops for a moment, as if to collect herself. "And then, when the war began in earnest, I realised I must do something. Talk to the dragons that remained, talk to King Luka, if I could."

"And did you?" I think I know the answer already but I have to ask anyway.

"No. General Kaller saw to my continued silence and poisoned the King against me, whispering untruths so foul that I had no choice but to flee." The venom is clear in her words.

The General who ordered the poisoning of the water? Sahva's tail whips again and snaps down with a thump. *How did he stop you?*

Talme's mouth thins for a moment and she takes a shuddering breath. "Before we were able to flee the castle; before I understood the depth of Kaller's deceits, he had succeeded in capturing two of my three apprentices, with my third only escaping because she was ill on the day and not where they expected her to be. It showed him for the power-hungry, depraved, soulless man that he is, that he'd worked out how to kill them without the magic returning to me on their deaths. I couldn't believe that I hadn't seen it in him earlier and that our magic has been decimated because of my slowness."

She stops and closes her eyes, sucking in a shuddering breath. "Ten years, and the magic still hasn't returned. And I don't know if it will."

Sahva hangs his head, sorrow evident through our bond. And yet, I have no idea what any of this means. It is clear that she still has magic, and I bite my bottom lip, trying to work out why they're both so sad. Nothing comes to me.

"I don't understand." The words rush out, as if saying them fast will lessen the risk.

Talme's eyes narrow. "No, I don't expect you would." She holds up a hand to stop my angry retort before it starts. "You were a child when we fled. And Kaller has made sure that magic has become an evil in the minds of our people. Are you sure you want to know? Given that it will make you more of an outcast."

My hesitation lasts only a second. I'm an outcast anyway and I want to know the whole story, now that I know part.

I nod and she inclines her head. "Our magic takes hold only in women, as it has done for time immemorial. A sorceress, when she takes on her full power, will be then joined by three acolytes, selected by the magic and found within our realm. They have only a small amount of magic – enough to be able to learn the skills needed when their time comes. And if one dies, the magic returns to the sorceress before settling in another acolyte. It protects itself with the power of three."

I nod, imagining for just a moment, magic running through my system. Being able to protect the people I love . . . I'm so caught up in the daydream that I almost miss her next words.

"When the sorceress dies, the power goes to one of the three, and that acolyte becomes the new sorceress. And the cycle starts again."

"So when General Kaller killed the two and their magic didn't return to you . . ."

She nods. "If their magic did not return to me, if I were to die my magic may not find its way to the last acolyte. If that happens, the magic will be gone for good . . . And our country needs magic – it is part of its bones – just as the dragons' powers balance their land, ours would wither and die a slow death without magic. And so I hide, like a coward, because I cannot risk our land."

I suck in a breath at the thought of the land dying. And it's people with it. We've been through enough! "We need to stop him," I say. "Stop him, end the war and give your magic the chance to return. For things to be fixed!"

Talme snorts. "I knew you were naïve, girl, but I didn't realise how much. How do you expect to do that when so many others; others who have used strategy and cunning their whole lives, have not been able to?"

Honestly, I have no idea, but I grasp at the words that flow out of my mouth. "Perhaps because no one would expect it from me. I'm not a soldier, I'm not a sorceress, I'm just a *girl*."

"And what do you propose? That you're going to just walk into the palace, wander up to King Luka and tell him the truth? And of course, he'll believe you without question and rid the kingdom of General Kaller on your say-so; the man he trusts, who has been like a father to him when his own died?"

It is the start of a plan, Sahva rumbles. *Sage is right. She will not be seen as a threat. She is perfect.*

CHAPTER NINE

"I don't know if I can do it." There's no quiver to my voice, which surprises me because my mind is a jumble of what-ifs, and none of them are good.

"Of course you can," Talme says, her voice crisp, no softness or empathy to her tone. "If you want this war to end, if you want your brother to be safe, our land to be safe, you will do it because there is no other option."

"What if it doesn't work though?"

Then at least we will have tried. Sahva's head is close to mine as Talme watches her apprentice, Challi, dress me in the uniform of the court servants. *You will not be alone. I will be there with you, even if I will not be in dragon form.*

"And my magic will assist you." Talme casts her eyes over me as Challi steps back. "Just as it will Sahva."

"What if they find out who you are though? *What* you are?" I turn to the dragon, wanting to tell him that I don't want to lose him. But not in front of Talme. She's agreed to help us but I don't know her well enough to show her this.

I will be fine, Sahva says with one of his slow blinks. *You will not lose me. And I will protect you if it comes to that. We will try to stop the war but if we cannot, we will not give ourselves as its next victims.*

I want, with all my heart, to believe his words but perhaps I've seen too much death to believe that everything will be fine. I have to try though. For Gaiven, for Varunah. So, I nod.

Talme grabs my arm and spins me around, a tub of something in her hands. "I cannot put a glamour on you. With no magic of your own to hold it in place, it won't stay. But we need to cover your talon mark. It will set you apart before you get anywhere close to the palace."

Her fingers push into whatever's in the tub and then she's tracing the line of the mark on my face, the cream so cold that I flinch in surprise. She stands back when she's done, checking her work before nodding. "Good. Enough that people won't notice unless they're really looking and then they will only be aware that you wear makeup."

She holds up a mirror for me and I go to touch the place where my mark should be but she slaps my hand away before I can. "No touching. You'll wipe it off."

I can't stop staring in the mirror though. I look like me again – the Sage that was looking for her brother, the Sage before Sahva.

I am sorry for what I have made you, Sahva says and there is true sadness in his voice. It tugs at my heart, pulling like there's a leash wrapped around it, drawing tight.

"No." I touch the scales on his leg, feeling the warmth of them under my skin. "Without the mark I wouldn't have known the truth about the war. I wouldn't have had a chance to change things. And I wouldn't have met you."

He must hear the truth in my words because he lowers his head to touch it against mine.

"As touching as this moment is," Talme says, walking to her desk and drawing two pouches from within, "we have magic to complete." She holds out one of the pouches to me. "Put it around your neck for when you need it. It's a truth serum. Three drops only in General Kaller's drink. Any more than that will affect his recall. As we discussed, find him and the King together and have him tell the truth of what he's done. We need to trust that the King is a good man, as his father was, and that he will want to rectify the wrongs done."

It sounds so easy when she says it like that but I have doubts over how good our King is. What if he already knows all this and doesn't care? What if General Kaller's poisoned words have been too effective? Or if one of them is away? How long will we have to wait to find them together?

There are so many unknown factors that it curls my stomach with the possible risks. "Wouldn't it be better for Sahva to use his powers to command them to tell the truth? What if they're not drinking? What if we don't get a chance?"

It is harder for a dragon to control two people at once, especially one as strong as the General. Not impossible, but harder. And given that the King will be well protected, as soon as it was evident that I was trying to control the General, I would have to control the King as well, before he called for assistance. I will do it if it is needed but it is safer with the serum. And using my power to control will not convince King Luka that I am not a threat – that the dragons are not a threat. It will not inspire trust.

"No, I hadn't thought of that. You're right. The serum is the best answer." I take the pouch and put it around my neck, trying to not show on my face the questions that are still tumbling through my head.

"This one," Talme says, holding up the second, dark blue pouch, "is your glamour, Sahva. It will hold without faltering for six hours, and will then last another two hours but it won't be as strong."

"Six hours! Is that going to be long enough? What if we don't find them together?"

Talme shoots me a look that, no doubt, has stopped further questions in the past, but our lives are on the line, as well as the end of the war. And six hours is such a short window of time. When I don't look away, Talme sighs.

"Every morning when they are in the palace, the King and the General meet to discuss the war. I have reached out to a former friend who–let me assure you–expressed their shock and surprise in hearing from me. The King and General are both in residence at the moment."

I lick my lips and nod. There is nothing more then. This is our best chance.

She nods, as if she can see my capitulation, and turns back to Sahva. "It will be tied to your dragon magic so you will still have access to your power, even in human form."

She steps up to him, and after asking permission, touches the scales on his chest with her hand, eyes shut for only moments before she steps back again. "It is done. When you wear the amulet, it will be activated."

This will not be an experience I ever expected to have. But I thank you, Talme, for the use of your magic and I promise we will do whatever we can to end the war and save your magic. And then, you can restore Harrton.

She inclines her head, her eyes serious, and he nods once at her, like a deal has been sealed.

#

We leave the house on the mountains at midnight, hoping the cover of night and the sliver of moon that shows itself will let us get as close to the castle as possible without being seen. Talme gives me more of the makeup to cover the talon mark should I need it when we get there. I'm rugged up even more than I'd been when we'd first arrived at her home, so there's a good chance some of it will be rubbed off.

Not that I'm complaining about the amount of clothes I'm wearing. It'll be nice to get there with my toes still feeling like they're part of my body.

We fly through the night, Sahva's emotions getting stronger the closer we get to the castle. They flow over me, influencing my thoughts, and I clutch at the fur jacket Talme had wrapped around me, trying to steady the nerves that grow stronger the longer we fly. Trying not to imagine all the terrible things that could happen when we get there, which only succeeds in making things worse and instead, I sink into the jacket further.

Dawn is still an hour away when Sahva sets down in a cleared field, as far from a house as we can get. I'm amazed no one has seen us; a dragon so close to the King's residence, but we're at the opposite end of the country from the dragon lands. And the magic surrounding and protecting the castle, put in place by Talme when she was Sorceress of the castle, has been maintained by Kaller despite his loudly announced distrust of magic, which means it's been a poor target for the dragons to choose.

That the same magic has never been offered to ordinary citizens so we might have some protection makes my jaw clench. I'm not the naive young girl Talme accused me of being though. I know we're just fodder; numbers to be used to win without any thought as to who we might be as individual people.

"How far are we from the castle?" I ask, my voice soft in the early morning air as I dismount from Sahva's back.

An hour's walk, as a human. If we wait until dawn breaks, we may save some time by finding someone to take us in one of the carts humans are so fond of.

I snort at him. "Yes, well it's easy when you can fly everywhere. Don't dismiss how much easier they make our life until you've had to walk for hours in boots with holes in them." I stop, gasping as a thought comes to me. "We don't have clothes for you! When you're human! How could we not have thought of that!"

His rumble is soft in the morning air. *Rest easy, friend. It is a glamour only. I will still be my dragon self – my size and shape will be merely changed. Talme will have built the image of a human form with all that is required as part of the glamour – clothes, boots. Everything to create the needed illusion.*

I shake my hands out of their fists and nod at him, feeling stupid.

You have not been around magic before. It is natural to have questions.

Sahva settles in the field to wait for the lightening of the sky and I lean against his neck, nestled in the crook of his front leg as if it's something I've done for years. *Ask your question.* Sahva's voice is gentle in my mind and I smile at how well he knows me. *We have time before I have to use the glamour and I will hear if someone comes long before they see us.*

I look up at the stars still holding on to the night sky. "I was

85

just wondering if dragons were born with magic or is it something they develop?"

We are born with the ability but it does not develop until five years past the hatching of our eggs. My eldest whelp, Dahva, had only just started to practice hers. She delighted in setting fire to sticks. Any stick she could find.

The sadness is clear in his voice but pride and love are there too and I try to imagine what sort of father he must have been.

"You must miss them."

Yes.

One word but it holds so much emotion there's no need for him to say anything else. We sit in a comfortable silence until the birds wake, filling the air with song.

Time for the glamour, Sahva says, *before we are discovered.*

I stand, digging into the pack for the dark blue pouch. A necklace falls into my hand as I open the drawstrings, and I touch the black stone hanging from the cord. It's smooth and cool and absorbs the early light.

Obsidian. The best stone to hold the glamour. Come; press it to my chest in the same place Talme touched when she set the activation spell.

I step closer to him and place the stone against his chest. The effect is immediate. I take a quick step back when the transition happens, taking me by surprise. Only the man's hand – Sahva's hand! – stops the necklace falling away.

The human standing in front of me now is tall; tall enough that he towers over me but not so tall as to attract attention. Dark, thick hair in a similar shade to mine falls to his shoulders and a strong nose dominates his face. Grey blue eyes are looking at me solemnly and he looks to be the age my father would be now if he hadn't died.

Let us not break the glamour, he says, looping the cord around his neck and tucking the stone under his shirt. *It is disorientating enough to do it once. To be so small and so . . . fragile will take some getting used to. How do humans live like this and not be afraid of everything?*

"I guess because that's all we know. How is it that you can still speak to me in thought?"

I am still dragon, Sage. Even if I do not look it. Remember.

I shrug. "Of course. It's going to be hard to remember when you look like that though. Can you speak out loud as well? It will be easier to get into the castle if you can."

"Yes." His eyes widen at the sound of his deep, raspy voice and he smiles at me. "Well, that is a most peculiar feeling!"

I smile back. "It's nice to not have to look so far up to see you."

"Do not get used to it." He looks at his fingers and wiggles them as if he can't believe he's in charge of them. "Although I must admit, having opposable thumbs is a convenience I would be happy to get used to."

I check that the second pouch is still secure around my neck, and tuck it back under my servant's uniform. We stow the pack and the jacket Talme gave me under some bushes at the side of the field.

"Come," Sahva says. "Let us make haste to take full use of this glamour."

We hurry across the field, strewn with wildflowers and long grasses, and ten minutes later, come to a road, paved instead of dirt since we're close to the palace. A cart, laden with vegetables, creaks up behind us a few minutes later.

The driver stops when she sees my uniform, her eyebrows raised. "You're a ways from the palace."

"Yes," I say, turning my face to look ahead of us, although Sahva has assured me the mark is still covered under the make-up. "I came to get my father. He's going to start work in the stables and we thought to stay the night at home before heading back this morning."

She nods and then glances at Sahva. "A big strapping fellow, I see. You're not one for war?" There's a hint of accusation on her face and Sahva shrugs.

"I was wounded last year," he says, his voice with a raspy quality to it still. He touches his chest, as if that's where he was wounded, and all I see in my mind is the wound he had when he first marked me, his scales torn away. It's like a full circle moment. "They will not let me fight again. That is why I will be working with the horses."

Her face softens and she nods. "Yes, there are many fine men who are not as whole as they once were. But then, we have to hope that the King and the General still have a plan. Climb aboard then, both of you. I'll give you a lift. It's the least I can do."

We clamber up on the seat beside her and she smiles at us before clicking to the horses. I wonder, for a moment, what she'd do if she knew she was carrying a dragon rather than a man. And decide I'm glad we don't need to find out.

CHAPTER TEN

The palace looms in front of us. Built of white and black marble, it's a beautiful monstrosity that claims its space dramatically at the edge of a cliff, leaving only one side to defend. It dwarfs the town spread out in front of it and yet, as I watch, it's apparent that the residents are used to living in its shadow.

I'm conscious of not letting my jaw drop open or my head swivel from side to side since I'm supposed to work here already. Sahva's face is grim as he stares straight ahead, as if being surrounded by so many people is hard for him. Perhaps it is, but I don't have a chance to ask, not with the woman driving the cart next to us.

It's only as we get closer to the main gate of the castle, that the things hanging from the walls become clear. Everything in me is begging to turn my head away, squeeze my eyes shut, climb from the cart and retch onto the grass on the side of the road. But I stay where I am, eyes straight ahead, as if I've seen this a thousand times before.

Because hanging from the walls are bodies. Bodies with their own talon marks, bright red against waxy skin, wounds to the heart; others with no skin left but it's obvious that there would've been a mark there. Sahva tenses next to me.

"Here is fine," I say to the woman as we get closer to the main gates, my heart speeding so fast through its beats, it's a wonder she can't feel me vibrating. She frowns at me and I smile in what I hope is a trustworthy way. "We have to see my aunt before we go in. My father has a message to give to her."

"Yes," Sahva says, his voice harsh and tight. "I have a message I must give to her before I start work at the stables."

The woman brings the cart to a stop, although it's clear that she doesn't want to. Sahva alights first and I hurry to follow, not wanting to give her a chance to question us further. And wanting to get away from the wall and the people like me, hanging there. More unwilling victims of the war.

"Thanks for the lift. We appreciate it," I say, throwing her a smile that is more like a stretched grimace.

"Are you sure—"

"We must hurry", I say. "We don't want to be late on my father's first day." More lies make the web that much harder to keep intact and I want her to forget us as soon as possible

Linking my arm with Sahva's, I move towards the houses at the side of the road. There's silence behind us and I'm sure she's watching where we're going but don't turn around to see. Only the sound of the wheels rolling once more helps slow my heart to a level where it doesn't feel like it's going to explode. Not that I feel safe. How could I after being made so devastatingly aware of the risk we're taking? Just . . . unseen again.

"Are you well?" Sahva's voice is a harsh whisper.

I press my lips together and nod my head. I'm not but this is the choice we've made and talking about it won't make the images fade any faster.

Sahva squeezes my hand as if he understands. "Talme said we need to go to the southern gate."

I nod in agreement, thankful to have something else to focus on.

We make our way through the small alleys that divide the houses; all of them so close, I'm sure they'd be able to hear their neighbours talking. It makes me homesick all the more, for our house on the farm and the room we had to run around as children.

No one stops us to ask where we're going or what we're doing. They don't give us a second glance. Maybe the servant's uniform helps me to be invisible and there's nothing expensive or noticeable about the clothes that come with Sahva's glamour. Talme has done a good job. There's something very dragon-ish about the way he's moving, although perhaps that's because I know what's under the glamour. He strides forward, hands behind his back, and head jutted out, as if he knows his own strength and is prepared to meet any threat with a burst of flame.

After going down a number of dead-end alleys where we're forced to backtrack and trying not to panic about the time it's taking, we find ourselves in front of the gate we need. It surprises me that it's only manned by two guards but then, if there was going to be an attack in this war, it would be from the air, not from the ground.

The guards watch us with interest as we come to the gate, but don't see us as a threat. Their swords remain in their scabbards and while their hands go to the hilts, they don't draw.

"State your business," one of them says as we approach but he says the words like he should say them, rather than meaning them.

Smiling, which I hope will counteract the glower that Sahva is giving them, I take a step closer. I'm praying that his expression has just a dragonish quality to it, rather than a desire to pick a fight with the soldiers. I want to nudge him, or kick his shins, remind him that I'm here, but there's no way I'd get away with that without raising suspicion.

"I'm to return to my duties this morning and my father has been put on to work at the stables. It's his first day today."

"Show me your orders." The man turns to Sahva, his hand out.

My mind goes blank, and then, to make up for the pause, my thoughts start a panicked race. Talme didn't mention anything about needing paperwork! And while I know it's been ten years since she was at the palace, it's a big thing to forget.

We'll have to walk away; that's if they don't arrest us for not having papers when we should. And we'll never be able to end this war and Gaiven will go to the war zone and might be killed, and we won't be able to save the magic that Varunah needs . . .

I press my nails into the palm of my hand, trying to stop the spiral of thoughts. It can't be all lost, not this easily. "We don't have—"

You will let us in and will forget you have seen us. As Sahva talks with his mind, the dragon power rolls off him in a way that makes me want to sink to my knees, just as it did the first time.

The guard who spoke shakes his head, as if he's trying to clear his mind. The other one frowns in confusion, taking a step back as if to get further away from us, and drawing his sword halfway out.

Sahva's glower deepens as he looks at them. I know it's harder for him with multiple minds to control but at least there's only two and not a whole platoon of soldiers. *You will let us in and forget you have seen us. Now!*

The guard further back drops to his knees, his head in his hands. I remember how it felt when it was happening to me – the overwhelmingness of Sahva's commands – and a part of me wants to rush forward and help him to his feet. The other part of me knows this is necessary if we want to stop the war. I just hope no one's watching, wondering what we're doing to the man. Sahva must have the same thought.

Stand up!

The guard gets to his feet slowly, as if he's pushing against the order, trying to break free. It's a relief to see that the other already has a blank expression on his face. I'm hoping that means Sahva's control is working.

Let us pass. You have not seen anyone of our description enter. You will not remember us.

After what feels like far too long, the first guard's expression goes blank too, and as we step around the guards, neither look in our direction. They look . . . vacant. As if their brains are no longer functioning as they should.

"Will they be okay?" I whisper, glancing back at them.

"Yes." Sahva doesn't turn as I have. "Now that I have removed my control it should take but a few minutes for them to return to normal. They will not remember us but we must hurry so they do not see us again."

We walk with fast feet through the castle grounds, trying to not look obvious in our haste, and duck behind a tall hedge that hides us from the view of the guards at the gate.

"Are you well?" Sahva's eyebrows have drawn down into a sharp frown and his fingers bite into my forearm.

I frown back at him. This is the second time he's asked me that question this morning and, unlike last time, I'm not sure what he's worried about. "Yes. Why?"

His eyes flick away for a moment before coming back to me. "I know how you feel about mind control; how you reacted when I was inflicting it on you. I wish you to know that I did not enjoy that. That it was a means to an end only."

I put my hand on top of his, grateful for his respect. "I know. And I understand. If we're going to end this war, getting a guard to let us by with no lasting effects to them is the least of our worries. I'm happy you were able to do it."

He nods, his face clearing of concern.

"Come on. We're running out of time," I say, taking his hand and pulling him along.

"Talme said we need to find the Sorceress' entrance. We'll just have to hope that hasn't changed in the last ten years as well." His urgency is clear through the bond, as he'd be able to feel mine – or maybe there's no individual feelings at the moment, just joint ones, determined to get this war ended.

The castle grounds are already awash with servants performing their early morning duties; tending to the gardens, exercising horses, sweeping paths. Everything needed to make the life of the upper levels of our society easier. It makes me yearn again for the life I'd had as a child, where the chores we did were for my family and their safety and comfort. The thought is tinged with resentment however. Resentment that I've lost all of that, while this still exists, with all its beauty and ease, not even remotely touched by the destruction of the war.

While we walk like we're supposed to be there; just two more servants getting on with their day, there are times when we choose to hide and wait for the bigger groups of people to pass. Each time someone glances our way, my body tenses, waiting for them to call us out. I have to keep reminding myself that dragons are the enemy and two people dressed as we are, might create questions but not panic.

The time continues to tick by. And my heart is increasing in beat with every minute that passes.

The dark, wooden door, set into what looks like a small, rock-walled gardening shed is where Talme said it would be and the relief that races through me makes my body sag for a moment. I trace the carvings in the wood with my finger – the moon in the eight phases of its cycle. Proof we have the right place.

Sahva lifts his hand up, hovering it just over the wood. "I can feel the magic."

"Can you use yours to unlock it, as Talme thought?"

He shuts his eyes in answer and I watch, breath held, as he moves his hand gently over the wood. There's an audible click and he opens his eyes with a smile. "Our magics are not so different," he says, pushing on the door.

The small space is empty except for a hole in the middle of the compacted dirt floor and the ladder reaching down into its depths. If Talme hadn't explained what it was, there'd be no way I'd go down there. It has a sinister feeling about it but maybe that's just my imagination heightened by the adrenalin. At least, with the door shut behind us, we're hidden from view.

"It's a good thing you're not in dragon form," I say, eyeing the opening that looks only just big enough for an adult to fit down.

"If I were, I would simply fly in."

"And get shot down within minutes. Or taken out by the magic that Talme put in place that dragons can't manipulate."

"Yes," he says, gripping the handles of the ladder. "I would deem this a wiser solution."

I follow after him, down, down, the darkness covering the rungs the lower we go. There's enough light at the bottom to just make out Sahva's face and the tunnel in front of us isn't at all inviting in its blackness. I wipe my sweaty palms on the uniform pants and try to slow my breathing.

"I am here with you. You are safe," Sahva says, touching my arm and I nod, my mouth too dry to talk. It's not the darkness that's making my stomach twist but, instead, the thought of walking along the tunnel – of all the earth on top of us, pressing down, waiting to crush me. When Talme had mentioned this, there was an abstract thought that it might be hard but now I'm here, I'm not sure I can take the first step forward.

Sahva reaches up behind me, lifting a torch from its metal bracket on the wall. He breathes in, as if he's trying to suck all the air from the passage and then, turning away, breathes out again, fire coming in its wake, lighting the torch. The flame softens the shadows, at least.

"Creating fire is much harder to do in this human body," Sahva says and I try to smile at him. It must be enough to convince him, because he inclines his head towards the dark passage. "Are you ready?"

I shake my head. The muscles in my legs don't remember how to move. And yet, this is the only way . . . our only chance. For once, I'm grateful that Sahva understands my emotions without me having to explain them. He takes my hand, rubbing his thumb against the top of my fingers until the rhythmic touch calms my heart.

"You are safe. I am with you," he says again and then, with one step, and another, and another, leads me into the tunnel.

I follow him, stooping a little even though I don't have to, my breath coming in short, sharp pants. We move with speed, our feet beating on the hard packed earth. And although it's about making it into the castle in good time, I'm sure Sahva understands the need to get me through this as fast as possible.

I have no idea how long we walk for; all I can concentrate on is Sahva's footsteps, listening to them, counting them, following them, until there's a lightening of the shadows that goes beyond the fire of the torch. And when the set of stairs appear in front of us, my chest relaxes a touch and I can breathe somewhat normally again.

"You do not like being below the earth?" Sahva asks as he slots the torch into the bracket at this end.

I shake my head and stuff my trembling hands in the pockets of the pants, ready to keep walking, but Sahva doesn't move.

"Why?"

I sigh and look up at the ceiling. He's shared so much emotionally difficult things with me, it'd be churlish to want to keep this to myself. Sharing the bond; sharing each other's emotions, feels like it entitles us to more, somehow.

"When my parents and sisters were killed, and our house destroyed, Gaiven and I had gone down to the river to sail his new toy boat. When we came back and saw . . . well, when we saw what had happened . . . we fled to a town a few days walk away. We'd only been there a week, maybe, trying to find work and a place to live when three dragons attacked the town. Gaiven and I escaped to the cave system in the mountains surrounding it; it's where we'd been sheltering for the week. But we went deeper than we had before, scared that the dragons might find our cave. And we became lost in there – wandering around for days with only small amounts of water to drink and whatever we had in our pockets to eat. Gaiv was so scared, crying all the time, saying he wanted our mother. He was so little and I had to be strong for him, even though I wanted her too. It was only through luck we found our way out. I was sure we were going to die in there and no one would've known. No one would've missed us."

Sahva shakes his head and the sadness is easy to read on his human face, without the benefit of the bond to communicate our emotions. "I am sorry you had that experience. You showed great strength for a young one. Come. We must end this."

The stairs that lead us back up circle round and round and my calves are cramping by the time we get to the landing at the top. Not that I care. I'd rather have cramping calves at the top of the stairs than be stuck underground.

Another door, a replica of the first one, stops our progress and Sahva uses his magic again. It's only as its click echoes in the silence that I wonder if there'll be anyone waiting on the other side.

Sahva opens the door with such caution that I want to yell at him to hurry up. He peers around before swinging it open. The large room is empty, just as Talme thought it would be. Of people anyway. Of dusty things that haven't been used in ten years, it's absolutely full. Charts of the moon and stars hang on the walls, maps of our country next to them. Shelves are covered with sorceress's equipment – burners and vials full of liquids and matter I can't even begin to identify, stones, crystals and in the middle of the floor, positioned over a fire pit, is a cauldron that has been blackened from many years of use. My hands twitch with curiosity and I want to stand here and study the charts and maps. It's a shame there's no time.

On one of the shelves is a baton-sized piece of wood, a crystal affixed to the top. I'm not sure what it's for but I take it anyway, stuffing it down the back of my pants and pulling my shirt out to hide it.

Sahva raises his eyebrow at me and I shrug.

"I don't have fire to protect myself. At least it might give them a good headache if I need to use it."

He laughs, soft and low, and I square my shoulders. "Let's go find King Luka."

CHAPTER ELEVEN

The door leading from the Sorceress' room to the castle interior is locked with magic. It answers the question as to why General Kaller left all of this here and didn't fill in the tunnel. Sahva uses his magic again and I hold my breath as he opens the door, expecting voices to yell in surprise that someone is coming from the Sorceress' room.

The hallway beyond is empty save for one young boy, who's standing in shock watching us, eyes wide, mouth hanging open. The empty metal pail he's holding slips from his hands and rings loudly as it hits the floor. I'm quick to retrieve it, and hand it back to him with a smile that he doesn't return. At least he isn't screaming, I suppose.

"Are you the Sorceress?" he asks, his voice laced with fear. Of course it would be. He can't be older than ten or eleven; all he's ever heard is that magic is evil.

I shake my head. "No, I don't have any magic."

He takes a step back, like he's about to run and the panic expanding in my veins again makes me reach out to grab his arm before he can. Sahva clamps a hand over the boy's mouth and looks at him intently.

You will not remember seeing us. No one has come from this room. You will go about your duties like you always do and remember that you've had a good morning. That people have been kind to you.

The boy's eyes go blank and then he turns, continuing down the hall as if we're invisible.

I look at Sahva. "That was kind."

He shrugs. "He is a whelp."

I shut the door to the Sorceress' room behind us, not bothering to lock it. No one will expect it to be open and we might need a quick getaway. Or somewhere to hide. Making our way down the hallway, we come to a busier area, filled with servants following the morning routine.

Sahva walks behind me and I try to act as if I'm supposed to be here. Every nerve in my body is tight, making me walk strangely, and I wait for someone to call us out as fakes. People glance our way but everyone's so busy they soon look away again, fooled enough by our disguises and intent on what they're doing.

I glance at Sahva, feeling the same urgency in him through our bond. Talme told us how to get to the King's rooms but there's no guarantee he'll be there. And if he's not there, he could be anywhere in this huge castle. Or the castle grounds. Or the stables. I don't want to think about how much time we have left of Sahva's glamour. At least we know – from the hoisted flag at the front of the palace – that he's in residence.

We make our way down so many hallways I lose track, past

huge rooms filled with beautiful furniture, paintings with gilded frames, silver candelabras that hold beeswax candles, not the smelly tallow ones of the poor. The King's wealth is on display everywhere we go and my mouth gets tighter and tighter, thinking of how little we've had over the last ten years, how many times I wished I'd had enough food to fill Gaiv's stomach and make him happy, even if just for a day. One single, silver candlestick holder, sold in one of the bigger towns, would've been enough to feed us for months.

We follow the directions given by the Sorceress, reciting them under our breath like a mantra, although we have no clear plan for what we'll do once we're there and it's that fact that has my stomach twisting into an uncomfortable knot. Gods, I wasn't made to live the life of a spy!

The servant's staircase isn't as full as I thought it would be. Some are loitering on the landings, chatting and laughing but most must be at their work. Sahva pulls me into one of the alcoves leading back into the castle proper, holding a finger to his lips. I tuck myself in as close as possible to the wall and Sahva stands sideways to me, as if we're deep in conversation.

"There are two people talking further up the stairs. They are discussing maintenance to be done in the King's quarters." He cocks his head and, as much as I strain, I can't hear the conversation he's listening to. "Quickly!"

I'm puffing by the time we've run up the next two sets of stairs, and as we come to the landing, the man standing there, toolkit in hand, raises his eyebrows at us.

"You two are in a hurry."

I grin at him, and wipe the hair away from my face. It's only when his eyes narrow, hatred warping his features, that I realise what I've done and my hand goes back to my cheek; a reflex action which only calls further attention to my talon mark which no longer hidden.

He grabs my arm and goes to yell, but the adrenalin in my system makes me faster and I pull the baton clear of my pants and smash it over his head. He collapses to the floor, his toolkit spilling its contents in a cacophony of metal on wood. I stare at the wound on his head in disbelief, numbly watching the blood spill onto the floor, before dropping the baton as if it's shocked me.

Sahva, thank the Gods, is quicker to react than I am, and he picks up the man as if he weighs nothing, nodding towards the toolkit. "Pick them up. Quickly, Sage."

The urgency in his voice snaps me out of my paralysis and I fall to my knees, grabbing handfuls of tools and the baton with its now fractured crystal, shoving them into the bag, shuffling back as the man's blood oozes towards me. It's hard to breathe. Why did I do that? Gods, Sahva could've compelled him! And yet, all I could picture, in that moment when he'd gone to yell, was the mutilated bodies of the talon marked, hanging from the walls. And how it could easily be me.

Sahva returns as I stand, bag over my shoulder, hands shaking. The man's shirt is in his hands and he lays it over the blood, using it to sop up as much as he can. There's still some smeared over the wood but it's definitely better than it was; not so blood-like in the dull light.

"Come," he says and we hurry up the next flight of stairs and through the door there, emerging into a library. Sahva ducks behind one of the shelves and I follow him, not able to think or plan or . . . anything. He shoves the bloody shirt in a vase at the end of the shelves and I grab his hands.

"There's no blood on you!" I don't know why this is the thing I focus on. Better, I suppose, than thinking about the fact that I've killed someone.

"The glamour," he says, and I nod as if that makes sense in my scattered thoughts. He takes the toolkit from my shoulder and reaches for my shaking hands, watching me.

"Where did you put him?"

"In a storage cupboard," he says. "Behind some boxes but it may not be long before he is found. Are you well?"

I frown at him. "Stop asking me that."

He lets go of my hands to grip my arms. "We must hurry, Sage. But I can feel your shock through our bond. And I need you to be settled. Thinking clearly."

I stare at him, trying to absorb his words. "I killed him, didn't I?"

Sahva's eyes are intense and his hands squeeze my arms in support. "Yes."

The air whooshes from my lungs and I sag in his grip.

"Will you let me settle you?"

"What?"

He taps his chest. "Our bond. I can calm your emotions but will only do this with your consent. And only because our time is limited."

I give a jerky nod, wanting more than anything to feel like myself again. Not because I'm okay with killing the man but because Sahva's safety is my responsibility too and I need to be able to think.

As if I've sunk into a warm bath, my muscles relax and the emotions settle within me. "Thank you."

He does his long, slow blink and it's that action that reinforces how much is at stake here. He is a dragon in the castle and will be killed instantly if found out. And I can't be the reason we're found. I dig into my pocket for the make-up that Talme gave me and smear some on my cheek.

Sahva's fingers stroke it over my skin and he steps back once he's done. "Good. Come."

We go back the way we'd come, and I don't look at the smear

on the floor. At least, no one else has yet noticed and sent up an alarm.

It's another twenty minutes before we reach the monarch's quarters and the adrenaline is pumping through my veins again, quickening my breathing.

The white and gold doors mark King Luka's private suites, just as Talme described. I can't believe no one else has tried to stop us, but then humans are not the enemy and no one has tried to assassinate the King.

The two guards standing in front of these doors however, are more alert than the ones at the gates. They stare at us, faces impassive, with backstaffs held across their chest, ready to be used, and swords hanging at their sides.

I clear my throat and gesture to the toolkit over Sahva's shoulder. "The King sent for someone to clean up a water leak in his bathroom," I say, concentrating on keeping my voice steady and matter-of-fact. "And someone to fix the leak itself."

The guards look at each other and then at Sahva but they don't move. "Fama is the maintenance man for the King's residence. Why isn't he here?"

I attempt a smile. "He took ill this morning. He's still in the lavatory, I think. We got assigned instead."

The guard narrows his eyes at Sahva. "I haven't seen you before."

Sahva stands taller and looks at them like they're stupid. I'm not sure if it's wise to antagonise them but have to trust that he knows what he's doing. "I am usually assigned to the lower levels so you, as the King's guards, would not have seen me."

The other guard snorts. "You talk fancy for a handy man."

Sahva doesn't respond - just inclines his head towards them. *Come here.* The compulsion is in his voice again and I steel myself against it. It's easier, the more he does it. I'm not sure who he's talking to though, until a woman in a beautiful blue dress, blond hair held up in intricate waves, comes around the corner.

The guards nod their heads to her. "Lady Almer."

I'm surprised they don't notice the vacant look in her eyes but perhaps they're just too polite to say anything.

Tell them you need assistance around the corner.

"I need assistance around the corner."

They look at each other and one of them shrugs. "Of course, Lady Almer."

Go. And when you round the corner, you will faint.

She turns and walks away, not looking at the guard who's now following her.

The guard remaining looks at us, eyes narrowed. "I'll have to talk to maintenance. Check out your story."

I shrug. "Sure. It sounded urgent though. But if it's okay to keep the King waiting . . ."

The other guard's cry of alarm reaches us from around the corner and I'm assuming Lady Almer has collapsed. I try not to smile. The guard's eyes flick down the hallway and then back to us.

He grimaces. "In and out. You've got thirty minutes before we come looking for you. The King is *not* to be disturbed. And we'll be searching you when you come out, so don't even think about taking a souvenir."

I bob a small curtsy as I pass by and then, unbelievably, the doors close behind us. I let out a long, slow breath. The area in front of us is twice as big as my family's home, and has a staircase that goes up at least three stories.

"This is a large living space for one man?" Sahva asks, his voice hushed. "He does not have a wife, is that not so? Or whelps . . . children?"

I shake my head. "No, it's just King Luka."

Sahva raises his eyebrows but doesn't say anything else.

"Where do we go?"

My words are interrupted by a man dressed in the King's livery, standing at the top of the stairs on the level up from us.

"You there," he says, pointing his finger at us. My chest squeezes, ribs pressing in. This is it. The rope is already tightening around my throat and every muscle in my body tenses, but then, the man turns away, still talking. "The bathroom is this way."

He doesn't look back to see if we're following but we hurry up the stairs after him. I'd smile at Sahva but the stress coursing through my body doesn't allow for it. We follow the man to the end of a long hallway where he opens a door and turns back to us.

"Hurry up about it. The King will be down in half an hour and I expect you to be finished and gone by the time he arrives. He has a morning of meetings. Get this mess cleaned."

And with that, he leaves.

The bathroom *is* a mess, the floor covered in water, and I hold my pants up as I slosh my way in. "Do you know how to fix this?" I wave in the direction of the tap that has water pouring from it.

Sahva snorts. "Plumbing is not something dragons have to worry about." He puts his hand over the metal of the tap though, and his magic rolls through our connection. In seconds, the metal has become hot enough to manipulate and he squeezes the faucet closed, stopping the water.

"It will not pass inspection but will not cause further damage. We must find where the King holds his meetings."

We leave the toolkit, hoping that on a quick review, it might look like we're coming back, and follow Talme's instructions to make our way to the King's study. No one stops us and when we slip through the door, I let out my breath and look around the room.

A large desk, devoid of anything other than a set of pens, dominates the space. It's too open to hide behind, and the bookshelves that line the walls don't offer any opportunity either.

A large fireplace is at the other end of the room and Sahva stalks over to it, narrowing his eyes as he watches the flames. "This may come in handy."

I'm not sure what he means but it doesn't matter at the moment. If he has a plan, that's great. All I can think about is that we need a hiding space in a room that doesn't offer a lot of options. The blue velvet couch near the windows is the only real possibility. We push it forward a little to be able to squeeze behind it, hoping the King won't notice. It's not comfortable, the two of us squashed in such a small space, but then we aren't planning to be here long.

It's only minutes before the door opens on well-oiled hinges and two sets of footsteps echo on the marble floor.

"This is the itinerary for your meetings today, Your Majesty."

"Thank you, Xavier." King Luka's voice is deeper than I expected but then, he's not the seventeen-year-old he was at the beginning of the war. "When am I to meet with General Kaller?"

I shoot a quick look at Sahva and he smiles at me.

"He is your third meeting for the day, Sire. I believe he returned from the front late last night."

I stifle a moan at the thought that our luck was cutting it so fine. Talme's information was not as good as she'd thought.

"Good, good." There's a rustle of paper and then the King speaks again, as if to himself. "Master Secclar will be complaining again, no doubt, about the amount of grain we're using to keep the army fed with so few able bodies to tend the fields. Why does Lady Almer wish to meet with me?"

I look at Sahva, eye's wide. The lady in blue that we used to distract the guards! Hopefully, she'll have recovered enough to attend the meeting and not create further questions.

The aide clears his throat. "I believe, Sire, that she wishes to invite you in person to her annual ball. I did explain to her that she would be unable to bring her daughter with her this morning and I will ensure that it's only the Lady who receives an audience with you should she choose to ignore that request."

"Ugh, spare me from ladies who wish me to marry their daughters. Especially ones who are eleven years my junior."

"Yes, Sire. Although, if I may be so bold, it would be a good alliance. Sir Almer is one of General Kaller's main opponents – having him in line would dispel a lot of the opposition to the war plans."

"Hmm." There's no enthusiasm in the King's voice and I wonder what that means. Not that I'm used to the political intrigues of court – nor would I wish to be.

Thankfully, the first two meetings are short but despite this, my legs are cramping in the confines of the small space. As Lady Almer leaves, having issued the invitation to her ball and recovered from Sahva's compulsion, the King rises from the chair he's been sitting in.

"Thank you, Xavier. You may leave now. I wish to speak to General Kaller on my own. Is his favourite whisky on hand?"

"Yes, Sire. In the decanter on the small table." I throw Sahva a startled look. It's the table closest to the lounge and if I wiggle around, I might just be able to put the drops in without them noticing. Moving as quietly as possible as Xavier continues talking, I'm careful not to jostle the couch.

"Would you not like me to document the meeting, Your Majesty?"

"No, that will be all. You may show General Kaller in."

"Very well, Sire."

The door opens and closes again and the King's footsteps tap out a rhythm as he paces the room, back and forth in rapid steps as if agitated. I wedge myself in tighter between the wall and couch to give me extra balance and pull the pouch from under my uniform, opening it and withdrawing the small, cold vial. My shaking hands make it difficult to unscrew and, for one heart-stopping second, I almost lose my grasp on it.

Then, waiting until the King's footsteps move away from us – with my heart pounding so hard against my ribs I'm sure he'll be able to hear it – I raise my hand to the decanter. And stop. How many drops should I risk? Talme said more than three would cause problems. I'm frozen, unsure and all I can think is that our chance is passing with each second.

In the glasses. Three drops in each with a hope that the King will not notice.

Sahva is right. It's a risk but the cups are made from an amber glass, and perhaps, the tiny amount of liquid needed in the bottom of each won't be noticed.

I reach out, tongue between my lips, concentrating hard to stop the shaking of my hands. Three drops fall into all four glasses. It's done. I recap the vial and focus on calming my breathing so that my gasps don't give us away. It's only moments later that the King's joined by a second person and his pacing stops.

CHAPTER TWELVE

"Ah, General Kaller."

"Your Majesty," General Kaller says, his voice deep and gravelly. If I didn't know what he'd done, I'd say he sounded like someone you could trust; someone in charge. "I'm glad I could see you so soon after returning from the front. There is much to report. But you wished to speak to me alone?"

"Yes." The King is pacing again. He stops after a moment and moves over towards the couch where we're hidden. I press back further into the wall, even though it makes no difference in him discovering us or not.

I am here. Sahva's voice is calm and I let it wash over me, shutting my eyes to ground myself.

"Would you care for a drink, General?"

"It's still early, Your Majesty." There's a note of disapproval in the General's voice and wonder at the relationship he has with the King, to be able to talk to him like that. Talme must be right about the power the General wields.

There's a pause but the decanter clinks anyway and there is the splash of liquid in a glass. My heart does a trembling flutter – he hasn't noticed the serum. Now they just need to drink. Please, oh please, drink the whisky! I press my tongue against my lips to make sure I don't say the words out loud.

"Still . . ."

The General sighs. "As you wish, Your Majesty. I will be pleased to have a drink with you."

"Good man." Liquid sploshes again and King Luka picks up two of the glasses before turning. There's so much energy running through my body that it's hard to stay hidden behind the couch; fear that the General won't drink but instead, will just hold the glass to humour the King, makes it worse. I want to leap up and hold the liquid to his mouth, ensuring he drinks, but squeeze my fingers together instead.

"Was there something in particular you wished to talk about without there being a record of it, Sire?"

"Yes." The King clears his throat and resumes pacing. "Yes. Well, it's like this, General. We can't keep this up. Our armies are being decimated. At this rate, we won't have any able-bodied men left when we defeat the dragons to rework the land and bring us back to prosperity. I've had Master Secclar here already this morning, complaining about the grain the army is using and the lack of crops for our next season because there's no one to work the fields. We need to get this finished. One quick routing of the dragons."

"Your Majesty," the General says, his voice soothing as if the King is an agitated child. "We're getting closer and closer each day to defeating the dragons. The threat of their magic will no longer be a problem and your kingdom will thank you for many years to come for protecting them from the scourge that's threatened our doorstep for such a long time. We are close, Sire, and we have sacrificed so much but we must be cautious, lest everything be undone. The next attack will be on dragon land, forcing them further back, attacking their whelps as a way of hobbling them."

Sahva stiffens beside me, anger and grief rolling off him in waves through our bond, and I touch his hand with mine. He flinches and then takes a deep breath, grasping my hand in his as if that is the only thing keeping him from jumping up and flaming the General to death. Satisfying, perhaps, but it won't get us what we want. And it won't make the King listen; only prove what he already believes about dragons.

"My father never had to deal with this," the King says and for a moment, he is the petulant youth the General treats him as. He clears his throat and, in the pause, the sound of him drinking reaches us. Has the General drunk yet? Talme said it would take affect within minutes, but what if the man doesn't drink at all?

I take in a quiet lungful of air and lean out from behind the couch. The King, broad-shouldered and dark-haired with a face still largely unlined, is pacing on the other side of the room now, and the General stands facing him, side on to us. He isn't as tall as the King but he's stocky, his body full of power and strength. Greying hair, cut short, and the sagging of his jowls are the only evidence of his age. His glass is full.

And then, as if my will makes it happen, he takes a sip. Not a big one but the Sorceress assured us it wouldn't take much.

"No, Your Majesty, he did not have the difficulties you've faced and yet, you have faced them like a true regent," the General says. "You are the king of your century and your people are lucky to have you and your perseverance in this battle that we couldn't foresee after our centuries of peace."

I wonder how the King can't hear the falseness in General Kaller's voice – the derision. It's obvious to me that he believes he can control the King; flatter him with compliments and keep him compliant, but I suppose, the King has trusted him for a long time.

King Luka snorts. "I'll be king of nothing if this war continues. My people are in pain, Kaller, and we need to finish this war and finish it fast."

"I know, Your Majesty."

The King bangs fist against the top of the chair. "You treat me like a child but I'm twenty-seven. Old enough to lead an army, as my father did."

"We've had this discussion before, Your Majesty. Your father was never in a battle against dragons. If you were out in the field, the dragons would be better able to attack you; control you. And that not only puts you at risk, but your army and your people as well."

"I think *you* just want to control me!"

The King's eyes widen, as if he can't believe what he's said and the silence hangs in the air, like a weight about to come down and chop off heads.

"Your Majesty, I *do* control you." The General stops, his hand going to his throat as if he's choking on something. I hope it's more words. "I run this country better than your father ever did and that's what I've been doing ever since he died."

The King's mouth is hanging open and, in silent agreement, Sahva and I rise as one. Our appearance from behind the couch would've been comical, exacerbating the surprise already on their faces, if it wasn't so important.

"Who the devil are you and what are you doing in the King's library?" The General reaches for his sword, stepping in front of the King. There's a part of me that respects him for his first instinct of protection, but the cynical side of me is in no doubt that it's to ensure his own continued power.

"I am Sahva and this is Sage." Sahva gestures to me, coming around from the back of the couch. "And we are here in peace; here only to make sure the King knows the truth of the war."

"Stay back!" The General holds his sword out as we approach and we stop, Sahva with his hands out in front of him.

"I assure you, we are not here to hurt the King in any way," he says. "We are unarmed, as you can see."

Well, except for magic and the ability to breathe fire, I think, but I'm smart enough not to say that out loud.

"What truth would you have me know?" The King moves around the General, who's scowling at him. "Why the war is dragging on, perhaps, despite the General's claim that it will soon be finished? Why he keeps me away from the fighting? From my armies?"

"Don't listen to them, Your Majesty. They're obviously here to make you doubt what I've told you."

"I *do* doubt what you've told me. All the time. I believe you tell me only what you want me to hear so as to keep me under your control." The look of surprise is back on the King's face but he squares his shoulders as if he's decided to own the honesty, and looks at us. "What do you have to tell me?"

"Your Majesty," the General says, his voice loud now. "Do *not* listen to them. You will do what I say! I don't want you to hear them."

"I don't care, General. Speak," the King says, holding out his hand to us.

Sahva glances at me and I nod, encouraging him. "What do you understand of how the war started, King Luka?"

The King frowns. "What do you mean? What's that got to do with how this damn war can be finished?"

Sahva's face stays impassive. "It has everything to do with ending the war, your Majesty."

"Your Majesty, this is ridiculous. You can't seriously be going to listen to this lunatic. I must insist that you stop–"

"Shut up, General, before I eject you from this room." The King takes another sip of his drink and stares at Sahva for a moment, before answering his question. "The dragons attacked an unarmed village on the border with no provocation. Killed men, women and children who had done nothing to deserve it, despite our treaty. The treaty which had existed for centuries. General Kaller believed it was because my father had died and I was a young king, hence they wished to take advantage of our momentary weakness and have power over us."

And we know, from the serum, that he believes this to be the truth. The General growls, as if he wants to say something but doesn't trust the words that will come out of his mouth. His hands are clenched, his eyes hard, and I want to pull Sahva back, get him further from this dangerous man, but I can't interfere. Not when King Luka is talking to us.

Sahva inclines his head. "A good story, Your Majesty, but that is not the truth. Before the attack happened on the human village, the dragons were poisoned – thousands of them, by the magic of Sorceress Talme."

"Ha!" The General's voice is harsh. "You see, your Majesty.

123

Magic is the cause of the evil that's befallen our country. That is why we had to root it out ten years ago; get Talme away from you before she poisoned you against me. Just as we will kill the dragons until there is no magic to defeat us; to bind us!"

King Luka turns to the General, a frown on his face as if he is contemplating the truth in the man's words. My heart leaps in my chest in protest and I want to shout at them to listen, but Sahva is already continuing his story, as if the General hadn't spoken.

"She did not know how the magic would be used, however, until after the horrific deed was done. Thousands of dragons, whole families of males, females and whelps, succumbed to the poison. The decision to use the magic to poison the dragon's water source was made by General Kaller, without your knowledge. That was why the dragons attacked – as revenge for the decimation of their population."

The King's frown deepens and he places his glass on the table beside him. "No. No, that can't be true. It's impossible. I would've heard something about it – would've heard rumours at least, at some stage over the ten years. The General could not have kept that from me. It's not possible. It can't be."

"Your Majesty," says the General. "I have always given you the information you need to know. Eject them, Sire, now! Before they say anything else."

I take a step forward, holding up the vial Talme gave us and, taking a deep breath, rush my words out. "This is a truth serum, Your Majesty. Made by Talme and given to us with her consent before we came here. Both you and General Kaller have taken it in your drinks. Ask him. Ask him if what Sahva told you is the truth."

The King looks at his drink, still sitting on the table, with shock and takes a stumbling step back from it. The General's glass shatters on the fireplace as he flings it from him.

"They came to kill you, Your Majesty. Poison you! Just as I said. Come, let me take you away and make you safe."

"If we had wanted to poison you," Sahva says, his voice calm, "we would have done it without showing ourselves."

King Luka looks from his glass to first Sahva and then me, as if in deep thought, but his hands have a noticeable shake to them. After a moment of silence, he turns to the General, his eyebrows drawn together, his face grim.

"Well, General, is this story true?"

"Your Majesty . . ." The General's face is a muddied red but it's obvious he doesn't want to answer. "Your Majesty," he says again, his words petering out once more.

The King's expression hardens. "Is. It. True? Yes or no? Did we poison the dragons, as this man has said? Were we the ones to first break the treaty? To have so many of our people killed in this blasted war?"

General Kaller growls again, shooting us a murderous glare. His mouth is moving as if he's trying to change the words waiting to come out.

"Yes! Alright! Yes, we poisoned the dragons and it's a decision I'd make again. Kill the lot of them, if I could. Your father was too weak to understand what needed to be done – to rid the world of their filthy, devil-given magic, holding power over us, holding land that should've been ours. But with him dead, and you only seventeen and so trusting – it was the perfect opportunity. And I took it!"

King Luka sinks into the chair behind him as if his legs can no longer support him, and stares at the carpet. "We started this war," he murmurs, the shock and grief easy to hear in his voice. "We're the reason for all this death – both dragons and our own people. We've given them all a death sentence by perpetuating this cycle of revenge and hatred."

"Yes, yes, and it's too late now to do anything about it. We need to continue until all the dragons are dead and we're safe. They won't listen to us now without requiring us to give all our power away which is, quite frankly, out of the question. We must finish it."

The General is standing tall again – a man sure of himself. Sahva's hatred through our bond matches my own. Most of my family are dead because of this man and he refuses to see what his decisions have brought. No, that's not right. He sees; he just doesn't care.

I wait to see if Sahva will say anything but he's watching the King, waiting to see what his reaction will be. His face is impassive but strong emotions are rolling off him.

King Luka shakes his head, as if he can't believe all he's heard. He's silent for another moment and then looks up, his expression grim. "We need to try to find a solution to this, despite the death and destruction that has already occurred. I won't keep my people at a war which is our fault. I won't have them dying still when there was no need for it in the first place. We were at peace with the dragons for hundreds of years. They didn't have power over us. They were separate from us."

"That's not possible. You're being stupid." It isn't lost on me that General Kaller is no longer calling the King by his title. From the slight tightening of the King's mouth, I'm guessing he's noticed it as well. "The dragons will never listen to us. What do you think you're going to do? Just wander into their lands and ask for a parley? They'll have you under their control so fast you won't have a chance and then they'll wipe out all of us. Don't be naïve."

Sahva takes a step closer to the King. "Would you really wish this? A parley with the dragons? An end to the war?"

The King meets Sahva's eyes, his gaze unwavering. "Yes."

Sahva nods at him, as regal in bearing as the King. "There is no need to go to the dragons, Your Majesty. One of them has come to you."

Chapter Thirteen

Both men are still; as if they're trying to make sense of Sahva's words as he bows at the King.

Then, General Kaller laughs. "You see. This is just ridiculous. A madman is the support you have. I suggest, *Your Majesty,* that you leave what you don't understand alone and let those who do understand politics and war get on with things. You are the perfect figurehead – young and good-looking. Let the men make the decisions, hmm?"

The King ignores the General – my estimation of his intelligence is going up – and instead, continues to stare at Sahva. "What do you mean?"

"King Luka, allow me to present myself. I am Sahva Sureclaw of the Black Dragons. I carry on me a glamour made by Sorceress Talme which allows me to have this meeting with you." Sahva's hand touches the amulet. "If I were to take it off, I am afraid I would wreck your library when I assume my dragon form. And I offer to be your messenger to the dragons if you would so have it."

The General makes a derisive snorting sound and the King frowns without looking at him.

"How do I know that's the truth? *You* haven't drunk the serum. Perhaps you are a madman, as General Kaller says."

Sahva inclines his head, acceding the point, and gestures to the lit fireplace. "May I?"

At the King's confused nod, Sahva steps closer to the fire. Which also brings him closer to the General. A burning worry engulfs my stomach and I move forward.

Settle, Sage. I am safe, he says and I stop at his words. But the worry still scalds my insides, as if *I'm* about to breathe fire, and I don't step back.

He narrows his eyes and then sucks in a lungful of air. As he does, the flames in the fireplace rush into his gaping mouth in a long, burning stream, until the fireplace is just ash and smoke. There is no movement from anyone, except from Sahva who turns to face us, his face impassive. A piece of charred wood falls into two pieces, breaking the heavy silence in the room.

"Well, that was impressive." The King is shaking his head, as if he can't believe what he's seen. "I'm assuming you can light it again?"

A small smile crosses Sahva's face and he turns back to the fireplace. He opens his mouth and breathes flame onto the charred wood that remains. Heat fills the room again, as does the slight sulphuric smell that comes with his flame.

"Dragon!" General Kaller hisses, lunging forward with his sword.

I react without thinking, barrelling my body into him. He's much bigger than I am; stronger too, but it's enough that it knocks him off balance and his sword clanks against the stone of the fireplace surrounds.

"Sahva!" I yell. He moves in front of the King, protecting him, although I'm not sure why. It's not the King the General was just trying to skewer with a sword.

"Guards!" The General's shout, full of authority, has the immediate effect of three soldiers bursting through the doors. "Your King is under the control of a dragon. Kill him and his traitorous accomplices now, before he wrecks everything!"

They stand mouths agape, swords held in front of them, torn between the King they've sworn to protect, and the General they've obeyed without question.

"Now!" Kaller's command propels the guards into action and they launch themselves towards the King.

"Stop!" The King retreats behind the desk, unarmed and unprotected.

Sahva growls at the guards, his dragon rumble vibrating deep in his chest. The guards hesitate for a moment, long enough for me to grab the poker beside the fire.

"Your Majesty," I yell, tossing the poker to him. Not a great weapon against a sword, but it is something, at least.

A guard raises his sword to the king, and Sahva lunges forward, driving his fist into the guard's face. He crumples to the floor like he's been hit with a mallet, face covered in blood. There's no way he's going to get up anytime soon. A momentary stab of pity for him compels me towards his fallen form. And yet, he did just try to kill his King.

The dying guard's collapse distracts the other guard long enough for the King to shove the poker through his chest. He reefs it out again and, oh Gods, there is so much blood! I flinch back, as if it's going to cover me.

The King reaches down to grab the man's sword and I yell a warning as the third guard slashes down, aiming for his neck. The King throws himself to the side, the sword only just missing him, as Sahva roars out a flame, engulfing the man in fire before sucking it back in to stop the flames spreading. The man falls to the floor, his skin blackened and the nauseating smell of burnt flesh filling the air.

I'm so caught up in the fight that I don't notice the General coming up behind me until his hand is around my throat, his sword pressing into my side.

"Dragon!"

Sahva whips his head around, a feral expression on his face.

The King, his face and clothes splattered with blood, stands taller. His eyes narrow as he glares at the General. "Kaller, let her go. Don't make this worse for yourself."

The tip of the sword pushes further into my side and I hiss at the sharp pain. Sahva stalks towards us and the General steps back, pulling me with him. "Stay back, Dragon! I will kill her. She deserves it, after all. Siding with the enemy."

Sahva says nothing. He stops walking but he doesn't look any less dangerous.

"Good." Kaller's smugness is easy to hear. "Now, you're going to take that sword you hold and kill the King. And once he's dead, I'll let both of you go."

There's no way he's going to let us go and Sahva's lack of movement shows that he recognises that too.

"Kaller." King Luka walks around the desk to stand beside Sahva. It shows a great deal of trust given what the General has just demanded of the dragon. "You've lost your mind. Put the sword down before there's any more deaths."

Kaller snorts. "You're in no position to make demands. You're a worthless King and a worthless man. So easily led. So easy to manipulate. It's me that's taken this country as far as it has. Clearing it of magic, setting us up to be the most powerful."

"Killing half of the population." As soon as the words leave my mouth, I know I shouldn't have said them. Why am I baiting him?

He growls in my ear. "Shut up, traitorous bitch!"

Sage, get ready to drop to the ground. Make yourself as heavy as you can.

I give the slightest of nods, heart thumping painfully against my rib cage, but I trust in him without qualification.

Now!

I drop, the sword cutting into my side as I do, but it doesn't matter. I fall out of the General's grasp and he stumbles forward. Sahva lunges at him but at the last minute, Kaller brings his sword up and it plunges into Sahva.

He roars in pain, and the intenseness of it through our bond has me roaring with him.

Sahva is on his knees when he turns his head. He draws a huge breath in, and then breathes fire out, the flame racing over the General's body. It's Kaller's turn to roar in pain but it's a sound I relish. If I could make flame myself, I'd join him in destroying the General.

And then, despite the overwhelming pain, Sahva stands again, sucking back the flame before it sets the room alight. The General's body, burnt beyond recognition, crumples to the floor.

King Luka steps forward, sword in hand. Without hesitation, he brings it swiftly down, beheading the corpse. "This is how we deal with traitors to the throne." His voice is rough with emotion.

I don't waste time looking at what he's done. Instead, I crawl across the floor to my dragon – my friend, who's collapsed beside the window. "Sahva," I say, gritting my teeth as the pain that isn't mine tears at me.

I must change, Sage. I must take the glamour off to heal.

Sahva's pain is clear and I know it'd take too much concentration for him to talk out loud.

"Yes," I say, even though I have no idea how to make that happen – no idea how to think around the pain.

"What can I do?" The King stands next to me, his brow furrowed. He says nothing about the death of the General, and it occurs to me that this might be someone I can respect. I hold up my hand, and he grabs it and pulls me upright, steadying me when I sway. My wound is nothing compared to Sahva's but the intensity of both makes my very bones ache.

"We need to get him outside so he can take the glamour off," I say. "We're bonded and he can use me to heal, but not with the glamour on."

"Bonded," he says, as if I've just confirmed what he's been thinking, but in this moment, I don't care what he thinks of me. I don't have time to deal with his prejudices or the brain space to explain all that Sahva has shown me.

"Help me." I bend over Sahva, putting his arm around my neck and try to stand but he's too heavy. Luka hurries to his other side and between us, we bring him upright.

"One flight up," King Luka says, and the muscles in his arms bulge as he takes most of Sahva's weight. He's no longer the grieving, skinny seventeen-year-old that needed to be led. "There's a balcony that should be big enough to take the size of a dragon. Although what the guards will think upon seeing one, I'm not sure. Nevertheless, I promise to protect you and Sahva."

I nod, unable to talk around the weight of Sahva, the pain, and my panic at the amount of blood that soaks into my clothes as I press against him. Sahva's face is white and I don't know what that means for him as a dragon, but it can't be good. Gods, I can't lose him. Not when we're so close to what we'd set out to do. We need him to be the envoy to the dragons but more than that, *I* don't want to lose him. The bond is a true bond. He is my dearest friend, whether in dragon or human form.

Hurry. The word is for both the King and I, and Luka stumbles at the touch of the dragon's mind to his for the first time.

King Luka grimaces at the sudden, unexpected discomfort, but doesn't stop and we're moving up the stairs, Sahva's feet dragging up every step. People are crowding around us, talking, yelling. I can't focus on what they're saying. I'm just concentrating on moving my feet; up one step and another and another. And then, we're moving through a large set of double, dark-wood doors, opened hurriedly by a man at the King's command.

The bedroom we enter is huge, dominated by a canopied bed, but I pay it little attention. The doors leading to the balcony are in front of us and I keep moving forward, the panic pushing me onwards. Sahva moans, and the sharp, iron smell of blood is all I can focus on.

The doors are opened before us again and I move past the

staring servants focusing on providing one last surge of strength to get Sahva outside.

As we cross the threshold onto the sunlit balcony, I collapse to the tiles, spent.

King Luka, drenched in sweat, lowers Sahva beside me. "What do we need to do?" The King is looking at me as if I have the answers but I don't. I don't! I suck in a breath, trying to think.

The glamour. I reach under Sahva's shirt and yank the stone from around his neck, ripping the cord that holds it. In an instant, the magic disappears, I have my dragon back.

King Luka gasps as Sahva's dragon form fills the balcony, and he steps behind me, pushed by a razor-sharp talon.

In the back of my mind, I realize that this is probably the first time the King has seen a living dragon up close. I can't focus on him though, or what he's thinking. All I can think about is Sahva. His breathing is laboured and the wound is just as bad as I thought it would be – despite his larger dragon size – and I'm reminded of when I first saw him.

"Don't die. Don't die." The words fall from my mouth with no thought as to who's around us to hear them, and I put my hand to his cheek, his scales still warm under my hand. "Take my strength. Take all of it. Don't die."

Sage. It feels like a goodbye, which can't be right. That's not how this ends. Not now. It can't be. I can't lose someone else.

"Don't die," I say again, and then, I succumb to the pain and the darkness.

EPILOGUE

The dragon shoots low over my head, black and blue scales glinting in the early morning sun. I look up at him, following his flight, smiling as he skims over the water and grabs a fish with his talons before soaring back up.

It's been just over twelve months since our audience with the King that changed everything.

Twelve months since the death of General Kaller.

Twelve months since Sahva almost died.

I'd woken much later that afternoon – on the balcony still – although someone had covered me with a blanket and put a pillow under my head. Sahva, beside me, was still alive but only just. I'd sat beside him, unwilling to leave, through the evening and into the night; a night where they'd bought out fire pits to keep us warm and the King had sat with us in an easy silence that I was grateful for. It took until the sun was sitting low on the horizon again for Sahva to heal.

He didn't need to tell me it had been close. That it'd taken a lot of energy from both of us, the damage received while in the human form much greater without his protective scales. I didn't try to understand the physics of the glamour, only grateful he'd recovered.

Things had moved quickly after that.

Sahva and I had sat with the King for hours. Wide-eyed servants brought platters of some of the best food I'd ever eaten for both the King and I; fresh hot-house fruits, spicy meats, crusty breads and a sweet treat the King said was called chocolate that I couldn't stop nibbling on, and uncooked slabs of meat and fish for Sahva. In this way, we were able to regain our lost energy while we planned how to end the war.

And then with the King's blessing and direct orders, I'd climbed onto Sahva's back and – to the consternation and shouts of people in the village – we'd soared from the castle, seeking an audience with the dragons.

For the most part, they'd accepted me as a bonded human better than Cadex had, especially when we talked to them of the ignorance, apologies and promises of the King, and proved that General Kaller – the instigator of so many deaths rather than Talme as they'd thought – was dead.

It helped, I think, that his death had been at a dragon's hand and that there'd been no punishment for Sahva from killing him. In fact, the King had publicly denounced the General to both humans and dragons; the man who'd led his armies for such a long time. It was a grudging trust the dragons offered after weeks and weeks of negotiation, but it was a start all the same.

We'd sought out Talme once again after our first rounds of talk with the dragons, flying her and Challi back to the castle to gauge what might be done to restore the magic that had been lost. The King had voiced his devastation when we'd told him what the General had done to the sorceress' apprentices and its effect on the magic. I was surprised at how quickly he'd accepted magic back into his castle but perhaps the betrayal from General Kaller made it easier to want everything to return to how it was before Kaller's treachery.

Talme, as promised, fashioned magic to fix the poisoned river in the dragon lands; part of the agreement negotiated. It'd taken a lot time, effort and magic, and both she and her acolyte took several months to recover.

It's only now, a year later, that vegetation once again covers the plains beside the once-poisoned river, burying the bones that had kept the dragon's grief on display. And the first clutches of eggs lay hardening in rocky nests – a new generation born next to their life giver to celebrate the end of the war.

Not that it's been without incident – there are dragons and people alike who've been unable to let go of the hurt and anger after so many years. They've been dealt with by both sides and for the last two months, at least, true peace is a possibility.

I'd seen Gaiven again and encouraged him to meet Sahva. The meeting had gone better than it might've before. Having the blessing of the King and being the instigators of the end of the war meant that it took a few hours for him to stop looking at Sahva and I with wide eyes but eventually, he'd turned back into my younger brother and had taken to teasing Sahva in the same way he did me.

It'd been hard to say goodbye, for Sahva as much as for me, but Gaiven was determined to be a doctor and I couldn't take that away from him. Didn't *want* to take that away, but I couldn't stay with him in Axiam.

While I'm no longer ostracized by my own people, I'm not welcomed either. It will take a long time, I think, for that to happen and truly, I don't much care for it as I once did.

My place is with Sahva. We've settled on the land the King gave us – us and the other bonded dragons and humans who don't belong in either territory. Bex and Hevil were one of the first bonded pairs who'd taken us up on the offer and it had been a full circle moment to speak with him and tell him all that had happened.

The beautiful tropical paradise where Sahva had brought me to bathe is ours now, between the swampy lands at the Northern tip of Varunah and the border of the dragon lands. My small cottage at the edge of the beach, a short walk from the springs, is my home. Mine. It feels nice to say it and I roll the word around in my mouth still, welcoming the feeling of peace it brings after such a long time of having nothing.

I don't know what will be in my future. Perhaps we'll stay here.

Perhaps Sahva will find a new mate or I'll find someone I can love. There's time though – lots of it. And for the moment, I'm happy to just be.

Time for dinner, friend.

Yes. This is more than enough.

ABOUT THE AUTHOR

A writer of copious amounts of words (because if they didn't come out, she's sure her head would explode), Sue-Ellen writes everything from heart-warming romances to young adult fantasies to picture books.

A best-selling, internationally published author, she's an eternal optimist who enjoys making things difficult for her protagonists, but loves a satisfying ending. She loves quirky shoes, dark chocolate and a good tea.

Sue-Ellen is on Facebook and Instagram, you can also find out more at her website.

www.sueellenpashley.com.au

ABOUT DEADSET PRESS

Deadset Press is an independent publisher of incredible speculative fiction. We provide publishing pathways for emerging writers from Australia and New Zealand, and aspire to shine the light on unique and diverse voices.

You can learn more at:

www.deadsetpress.com

ALSO BY DEADSET PRESS

Radcliffe by Madeleine D'Este

A three-storey ramshackle house in North Melbourne is full of secrets.

Tamsin is lead to the building by a voice inside her head that tells her 'Death is Coming'.

With no respite from the eternal summer heat, can Tamsin find out who death is coming for and solve the riddle of Radcliffe?

The Rise by Sue-Ellen Pashley

Katie James' life is about to change . . . Again.

Having survived the great rise which decimated the land, the former medical student has made a new life for herself under the leadership of the Authority.

But her peaceful existence on the edge of the Sunshine Coast hinterland is shattered when she discovers a body floating in the waves. Unsure who she can trust, Katie embarks on a mission to discover the truth . . .

Even if it puts her on the same kill list.